SPIRIT OF THE WITCH

WITCHES OF KEATING HOLLOW, BOOK 3

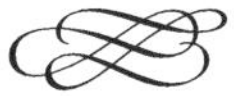

DEANNA CHASE

First Edition 2018

Cover Art by Ravven

Editing by Angie Ramey

ISBN Print 978-1-940299-67-9

ISBN Ebook 978-1-940299-68-6

Bayou Moon Press, LLC

ABOUT THIS BOOK

Welcome to Keating Hollow, the enchanted town where love heals, friends are forever, and family means everything.

Yvette Townsend's life was perfect...right up until her husband fell in love with someone else. Newly divorced and still reeling from her broken dreams, Yvette's sworn off men. Now she's determined to lose herself in her magic and her beloved bookstore. There's only one problem—she has an unexpected new business partner who's driving her crazy both at work and after hours.

Jacob Burton has always been an excellent businessman, but his track record with relationships is nothing short of tragic. After finding his fiancée in the arms of his best friend, he moves to Keating Hollow and invests the quaint bookstore to keep it from going under. But as time goes on, it becomes more and more clear that Yvette and the town just might be saving him. And if he's lucky, he'll find out what it means to love the spirit of the witch.

CHAPTER 1

Yvette Townsend stared at the man standing behind her desk, and desperately wished she'd been born an earth witch. At least then she'd have been able to spell the floor to open up and swallow her whole. Instead, since she was a fire witch, the only way she could magic herself out of this situation was by burning her beloved bookstore down, and that wasn't an option.

She'd just walked into her office to find Jacob, the man she'd had a one-night stand with two nights ago, talking about the big changes he wanted to make to her bookshop—correction, apparently, *their* bookshop.

He tossed the folder he was holding onto the desk and cleared his throat. "Maybe we could start over? Forget Saturday night ever happened?"

Her face turned so warm she actually fanned herself. Was he insane? There was no way she was ever going to forget the things he'd done to her.

"There's no need to be embarrassed," he said with a

chuckle, sliding out from behind the desk and walking over to her.

She glanced up at him and let out a startled huff. She wasn't just embarrassed; she was mortified. How could she have let this happen? Three months ago she was happily married and the proud owner of Keating Hollow's only bookstore. Now she was waiting for her divorce to be finalized. And because she'd needed to buy-out her soon-to-be ex-husband, she'd taken a deal with Michael J Burton, Miss Maple's nephew, to be her new business partner. Only they hadn't actually met in person while they were negotiating. Everything had been handled over the phone and through email. Otherwise she'd have never invited Jacob, the handsome, so-called bartender, back to her place the night of her sister's wedding.

Yvette narrowed her eyes at him, a surge of anger fueling her ire. "There's no way I could've known Jacob the bartender was really Michael Burton, the former regional manager of Bayside Books in Los Angeles. How is it you didn't know who *I* was? I was wearing a bridesmaid dress. And I know for a fact you knew I was Abby's sister when you took me home."

"I only knew you were a Townsend sister," he said with a shrug. "How was I supposed to know you owned this shop?"

She tsked and placed her hands on her hips. "Well, there are only four of us Townsend sisters. Abby was the one in white getting married. That meant you had a thirty-three percent chance you were jumping into bed with me."

Jacob's eyebrows pinched together as he reached into a messenger bag, pulled out a large envelope, and produced a set of documents. After a quick scan, he turned them around and pointed to her name. "It says here the owner of Hollow Books is Yvette Santini. Not Townsend."

Crap on toast. He had a very valid point. "Um, well, my

married name is Santini, but since my husband left, I've switched back to Townsend."

Standing entirely too close to her, he gave Yvette an apologetic smile. "I'm sorry this has created an awkward situation for us. If I'd known I was taking my new partner home, I'd like to think I'd have kept it professional."

"You'd like to *think* you'd have kept it professional?" she blurted out, taking a step back. "Is this a habit for you? Sleeping with your co-workers?" As soon as the words were out of her mouth, she recalled that the last business he'd run had been with his ex-fiancée. Their split had made the town's gossip mill since Jacob was Miss Maple's nephew.

Jacob leaned against the big mahogany desk and folded his arms across his chest. "I wouldn't call it a habit, but you can't blame me for being attracted to a gorgeous woman. And that dress…"

Yvette rolled her eyes. "It was a bridesmaid's dress. Those things are always awful."

"Not on you." That sexy smile that had lured her in the first time was back. "It's no secret I couldn't wait to get you out of it."

Her gaze shifted from his gorgeous dark eyes to his lips, and she practically swayed toward him as memories of Saturday night came flooding back. The clock ticked in the silent office as neither of them said anything for a moment. Then his smile grew into a self-satisfied grin.

Yvette held her hand up and shook her head. "This isn't going to happen again, and you need to stop this. If we're going to work together, there can't be anymore flirting. We're just going to have to pretend this never happened."

"I wasn't flirting," he said, trying and failing to look innocent as he swept his gaze down her body.

"Oh, come on." She rolled her eyes. "I'm not some silly coed who can be swayed by your adorable smile and that annoying twinkle in your eye."

He laughed. "If you say so." Then he was all business, standing up straight as he held his right hand out. "Ms. Townsend, it's a pleasure to meet you. I'm Jacob Burton, your new business partner. And I'm excited to see what we can do with Hollow Books in the upcoming months."

Yvette hesitated. Was he serious? He'd gone from frat boy to polished business man in less than two seconds flat.

"It's okay to shake my hand," he said with a hint of a smile. "I don't bite."

Yes, you do, Yvette thought, and she felt her face flush again as she clasped her hand in his.

"Much," he added with a wink and squeezed her fingers.

"Okay, that was definitely flirting," she said, pulling her hand back and placing her fisted hands on her hips.

"You started it," he said with a shrug. "Those red cheeks told me everything I needed to know about what you were thinking."

She averted her gaze and mumbled something about how his assumptions couldn't be further from the truth. *Liar, liar, pants on fire,* her voice rang in her head. He had her number, but she'd rather die than admit it. Yvette steeled herself, stared him straight in the eye, and said, "From here on out, our relationship is strictly business."

His damned eyes twinkled as he nodded and said, "Whatever you say, Ms. Townsend."

"Well, okay then," she said, itching to wipe her sweaty palms on her jeans. "It's nice to meet you, Mr. Burton." Yvette quickly moved and took her place behind her desk. After she sat in the leather chair her ex had custom ordered for her, she picked up the folder Jacob had dropped in the middle of the desk and waved it at him. "Now, about those changes you were talking about."

"Yvette!" she heard her sister Noel call out as her office door started to open. "Oh. Em. Gee. Spill. What happened with the hottie you took home after Abby's wedding?" Noel strode in and stopped in her tracks as she spotted Jacob. "Oh, oops. Uh, hello there." She brushed her long blond hair out of her face as she grinned at him and held her hand out. "I'm Noel Townsend. Abby's other sister."

He took two steps forward and shook her hand. "Jacob Burton, Yvette's new business partner."

"*Business partner*?" She glanced from him to Yvette and back to Jacob. "Well, this is awkward, isn't it?"

"Not at all," he said graciously and then turned to Yvette. "I'll be out in the store getting the lay of the land. Come find me when you're ready to talk strategy."

Yvette just nodded. The mortification had taken over again, and she didn't trust herself to speak.

"It was nice to meet you, Noel," he said then slipped out of the office.

The moment the door closed, Noel turned to Yvette, her eyes wide. "You slept with your new business partner?"

Yvette leaned back in her office chair, still holding the file Jacob had left on her desk. She cleared her throat. "What makes you think I slept with him?"

Noel gave her sister a flat stare as she tied her hair up into a haphazard bun. "Vette, come on. I saw you two leave together."

"So?" Yvette shrugged one shoulder. "Maybe he was just giving me a ride home."

"We saw that silver Mercedes parked at your house when we were on our way home Saturday night. Your lights weren't on. Please, there's no need to pretend with me. He's *H-O-T*, with a capital H. And after everything with Isaac… well, you deserved a little fun."

"I did, didn't I?" Yvette said, flipping the file open.

"Except…" Noel glanced back at the closed door. "I thought he was one of Clay's friends, a bartender from SoCal. Do you really think it's a good idea to get involved with your business partner?"

Yvette let out a sardonic laugh. "No. Not at all. I thought the same thing, that he was just a friend of Clay's. I just found out this morning that he's my co-owner."

Noel blinked twice and sat in the chair across from her sister. "What? How could you not know? Didn't you two talk at all?"

Yvette's face flushed hot again as she shook her head. "Not really. We flirted and then… well, you can guess what happened next."

Noel leaned forward, placed her folded arms on the desk, and gave her sister a wicked smile. "I could, but it'd be more fun to have details."

"Not on your life! Do I ask you about your antics with Drew?" Yvette asked, referring to her sister's deputy-sheriff boyfriend.

Noel laughed. "No, but last night we went skinny dipping down at the enchanted river. And I'm telling you, you haven't lived until you've had an org—"

"That's quite enough." Yvette held up one hand and laughed. "I've got the picture."

Noel sighed. "That river really is magic."

"You're depraved," Yvette said, scanning the notes in Jacob's file. She frowned and flipped the page.

"What is it?" Noel asked.

Yvette gritted her teeth. "When I walked in here this morning, Jacob was on the phone talking about the changes he wanted to make to my store. I heard something about a café and turning it into the premier paranormal bookstore on the west coast."

"That doesn't sound so bad," Noel said, her eyebrows raised. "What's wrong with that?"

Yvette dropped the paperwork and stared at her sister. "I'll tell you what's wrong with that… I *like* the store the way it is. It's quiet and quaint and the customers love it. Plus Mr. Let's-Change-Everything hasn't run one thing by me."

"Okay, so you talk about it," Noel said, shrugging one shoulder. "There's always room for improvement, right?"

"Talking would've been the place to start." Yvette stood, clutching the supply order in her fist. All the embarrassment from finding out she'd slept with her partner was gone, replaced by sheer aggravation. How dare he just come in and take over as if her business were in trouble? That couldn't be further from the truth. Everything was just fine. If it hadn't been for her impending divorce and buying out Isaac, she wouldn't have needed a penny from an investor. "It seems *partner* is a foreign word to Mr. Burton. Because apparently, he's already placed an order for a fancy industrial grade espresso machine, signage, and everything else one needs to serve coffee and pastries."

"Uh oh," Noel said, getting to her feet. "What are you going to do?"

Yvette stalked to the door then turned to look her sister in the eye. "Tell Mr. Fake-Sexy-Bartender to take his damned money and hightail it back to southern California. This isn't what I signed up for."

CHAPTER 2

Jacob wandered through the nonfiction section of Hollow Books and sucked in a deep breath, steadying himself. When he'd walked into the store this morning, the last person he'd expected to see was the sexy brunette he'd taken home on Saturday night. How was he supposed to know that Yvette Santini was one of Abby's sisters?

It wasn't as if he'd spent a lot of time in Keating Hollow, only a few summers when he'd been a kid. That was when he'd met Clay Garrison. They'd reconnected when Clay had moved to Los Angeles with his first wife, and Jacob had made a point of calling Clay when he realized he was moving to Keating Hollow. It had just so happened that Clay was getting remarried, and he'd asked Jacob to fill in as bartender at the last minute. Since Jacob had worked in a bar during college, he was glad to help.

He hadn't expected to take one of the bridesmaids home, but Yvette had thoroughly worked her way under his skin. She was hauntingly beautiful, a little sad, and a little rebellious.

What had started off as a harmless flirtation had quickly turned into something much more.

Jacob ran a hand through his hair and berated himself for his poor judgment. The minute he'd realized his mistake, he should've kept it professional. Instead, he'd flirted relentlessly and made an ass out of himself. It'd taken him all of forty-eight hours to throw a wrench in his new business arrangement. He could still hear his father's harsh judgment after his last failed workplace romance and the inevitable mess that followed. This time was supposed to be different. This time *would* be different if he had anything to say about it. He just needed to make sure he stayed out of Yvette Townsend's bed.

Too bad he had a feeling that would be easier said than done.

He needed to get his head on straight and remember he came to Keating Hollow for a fresh start, to lose himself in his work. Building businesses was his talent, and he had the record to prove it. He turned, automatically searching for his name among the spines on the shelves. Almost instantly, his gaze locked on the book his publisher had released the year before: *Loyalty Marketing: Creating Businesses with Heart*. If there was one thing Jacob Burton was good at, it was creating customer loyalty. And that's exactly what he intended to do at Hollow Books.

"Seriously?" Yvette said from behind him, her voice incredulous.

Jacob turned to her, still holding the book. "Pardon?"

"What were you planning to do with that?" She pointed to the tome in his hand. "If you think you're going to impress me just because your book made the *New York Times* list, well..." She shook her head. "Never mind. If you were planning on using that to convince me to open a coffee bar, you can forget it. That is never going to happen. And this,"—she held the supply order up and waved it in his face—"You'll need to send it all back."

Jacob gazed down at her, both slightly annoyed and amused. "What's wrong with a café? Readers like coffee and pastries while they browse book stores."

Yvette sighed. "I know you're from the big city, Jacob, so let me break this down for you. Keating Hollow is a small town. We take care of each other here. If you think I'm going to suddenly start competing with the Incantation Café, then think again. There just isn't room for two coffee shops in this town."

"That's fair," Jacob said with a nod. "But I wasn't suggesting opening a coffee shop, just an espresso station where it will be convenient to get coffee and lattes without having to walk a mile to the café. Your one-cup Nespresso machine isn't enough to accommodate specialty drinks for a crowd of customers."

"It's not a mile to the Pelshes' café," Yvette said with exasperation. "And really, who do you think you are, coming in here on your first day and making unilateral decisions on the direction of the bookstore? In case you didn't notice, Mr. Burton, Hollow Books does just fine. We don't need any fancy espresso makers to keep our customers happy."

Just fine? Jacob thought to himself. When was the last time she'd looked at the financials? He tightened his grip on the book in his hands and cleared his throat. "I thought you wanted to go into business with someone who would help your store grow."

"I did!" She placed her hands on her hips and fixed him with a determined glare. "What I did not expect was for someone to come in here and ride roughshod over me just because he made a name for himself turning his daddy's bookstores into a multi-million-dollar franchise." She waved at the book in his hands. "I already told you I'm not interested in turning my store into another Bayside Books."

"That's not—" he tried to break in, but Yvette was on a roll.

"You told me you were buying into my store because you were interested in a slower pace, something meaningful, and building community. Well, we already have that, Mr. Burton. We don't need any fancy espresso machines or your, quote, 'award-winning smile that can charm the pants off of every sales rep from coast to coast.' All we need is personalized attention and well-stocked shelves, just like your little book here says in chapter two."

Jacob's lips twitched as he tried to hold back a smile. She'd not only read his book, she'd memorized one of the quotes that was buried deep in one of the later chapters. He loved that she'd done her research on him. It meant he hadn't made a complete mistake partnering with her, even if she was being too stubborn to so much as listen to his ideas.

"Nothing to say, Mr. Fix-it?" she quipped.

"Sure. I have plenty to say, but I was waiting to see if you were done yet," he said with a shrug.

"I'm finished," she huffed out.

Jacob slid the book back onto the shelf and tucked his hands into his pockets. "You're right. I should have spoken to you before I ordered the espresso machine."

"Damn right," she said, keeping her expression neutral.

He ignored her jab and continued on as if she hadn't spoken. "The reason I jumped right in is because when I was going over the numbers for last year, it was obvious that the store isn't in trouble, but it will be if something doesn't change. I might've been a little overzealous—"

"What are you talking about? My store isn't in trouble," Yvette said.

"Yet," he said and rocked back on his heels, all of his

amusement at her outburst fleeing as irritation set in. This was business and if she couldn't be rational, this partnership was not going to work. "Listen, Yvette—"

"You *listen,* Jacob. I think I've heard just about everything I need to hear this morning. Thanks for considering investing in my store, but I think it's clear we're on two separate pages. It's probably better if we call this whole thing off and you just go back to Bayside Books or whatever it was you were doing before you got here."

Jacob blinked. Was she serious? They hadn't even had a full conversation about the store yet. And there was no way in hell he was headed back to Los Angeles. Not after everything that had gone down there. Like it or not, she was stuck with him… for now. "You can't just unilaterally decide this arrangement isn't going to work and toss me out. We signed contracts. Money has changed hands. I am the co-owner of this book store now." Fifty percent co-owner. He'd insisted upon that. In business, he was never silent. "We're just going to have to figure out a way to make this work."

Yvette frowned, her brow crinkling. "Contracts can be voided, and I'll find a new investor. One whose vision for the store is the same as mine. Thank you for your time, Mr. Burton, but it's pretty clear we've both made a mistake."

Then without another word, she turned and stalked right out of the bookstore.

He stood there in the aisle, watching as the door slammed shut.

Footsteps sounded behind him, and he spotted Noel moving toward him. Her wavy blond hair was spilling out of a messy bun, and even though she was just wearing ripped jeans and a T-shirt, she looked like she'd just stepped out of the pages of a fashion magazine. *There's no shortage of good looks in the Townsend clan,* he thought. Though, while Noel was pretty in an all-American-girl way, Yvette's beauty was less obvious. Her features were darker, more angular, and she was full of fire.

"That went well, I see," Noel said as she walked over to him, a sympathetic smile on her pretty girl-next-door face.

He let out a bark of laughter. "You must've heard a different conversation." Shaking his head, he added, "What kind of crazy did I just walk into?" The woman he'd spoken to on the phone had seemed bright, intelligent, and receptive to his early ideas on how to grow Hollow Books. The one he'd just met, well, irrational and defensive were the adjectives that came to mind.

"Listen," Noel said, putting a light hand on his arm. "She's been through a lot in the last few months. This bookstore has been the one constant in her life, the one thing that's still hers.

But it wasn't anymore. At least not all hers. Jacob had invested a significant chunk of money in the place, and he wasn't going to sit back and let it burn just because his new business partner was having trouble adjusting.

"Just… give her a little time," Noel said. "Trust me. She'll come around sooner or later."

Jacob met Noel's kind gaze and nodded. "Thanks."

"Sure. And welcome to Keating Hollow." She headed for the door, but just as she grabbed the door handle, she glanced back. "Jacob?"

"Yeah?"

"Be careful with her. She acts tough, but if you look closely there's no missing the heart she wears on her sleeve."

Jacob didn't answer as he watched Noel exit the store and disappear out into the streets of Keating Hollow.

CHAPTER 3

Yvette was fuming as she strode into her dad's brewery and hopped up on one of the stools at the bar. "Rhys, give me the tallest glass of Clay's New Year brew."

The broad-shouldered, handsome assistant manager glanced up from his clipboard and eyed the clock. "It's nine-thirty in the morning. We're not even open yet."

She glared at him. "Is the tap broken?"

"No." Chuckling, he grabbed a thirty-two-ounce glass and started filling it from the tap. "I'm just surprised to see you. Tough Monday?"

"You can say that again." She stood and disappeared into the kitchen. A moment later, she returned with a slice of berry pie that was covered in a mound of whipped cream.

Rhys placed the beer in front of her. "Want to talk about it?"

She shoved a forkful of pie into her mouth and shook her head.

"Got it. Let me know if you need anything else." He moved

back to the other end of the bar and resumed concentrating on his paperwork.

A time machine? Then she could go back and undo the mess she'd made for herself. First on the list would be to *not* go into business with Mr. Franchise. Second would be to *not* take him home after Abby's wedding. The only problem was no one had exactly been beating her door down to invest in the bookstore. In fact, Jacob had been the miracle she'd been praying for. If she hadn't been able to buy Isaac out, she'd have been forced to close and liquidate all of her assets. Then she'd have lost her marriage and her beloved business.

Her threat to buy back Jacob's investment had been just that. She didn't have the money. She owed too much on her house to leverage it and she'd already tried a business loan. None of the banks were willing to lend her that much. That's how she'd ended up with Jacob as a partner in the first place.

She picked up the beer and closed her eyes as she took a long, fortifying sip.

"Yvette?" Her dad's voice startled her, and she sputtered, spraying part of the beer on the counter.

"Dad? What are you doing here?" she asked as she ran behind the counter to find a towel to clean up her mess.

Her father was standing in the doorway of his office, the one that Clay usually occupied these days. "I was going to ask you the same question. I'm filling in for Clay while he and Abby are on their honeymoon." He glanced at her dish and raised one eyebrow. "It's a little early in the day for beer and pie, don't you think?"

"It's never too early for pie." She moved her plate and beer glass aside, sprayed the counter, then wiped up the spatter of beer. "You taught me that, remember?"

He chuckled. "I guess so, but I don't remember washing it down with beer."

"Some days it's necessary. Trust me." She put the towel away and retook her seat at the bar.

Her dad walked over and leaned on the counter. "Want to talk about it?"

Talk about it? Gads no. How could she tell him she'd slept with Jacob? There were some things that fathers never needed to know. She studied him, noting the dark circles under his eyes had all but disappeared and his color was normal again, not gray from the chemo. He was still too thin, but all things considered, he looked good. She'd always tried to remain positive that her dad would beat the cancer, but now, seeing him recovering, something inside of her was starting to let herself believe it.

Some of the tension drained from her shoulders, and she decided maybe he was the person she needed to talk to… just as long as she kept Saturday night out of it. "I think I've made the biggest mistake of my life."

Lin Townsend pursed his lips as he regarded her. "No wonder you're drinking before ten in the morning."

Yvette let out a sad chuckle that was half amusement, half sob. "You have no idea. I think this discussion calls for another slice of pie."

She started to slide off her stool, but her dad straightened and raised one hand. "I'll get it. Extra whip?"

"Yes, please," she said, pushing her empty plate toward him.

"You got it, Rusty," he said, using the nickname he'd given her when she was a kid. Of the four Townsend girls, she was the only one with chestnut hair. The other three were blondes.

While her father was in the kitchen, Yvette used the opportunity to refill her beer glass. Then she poured a cup of coffee for her father, knowing that would be his beverage of choice.

When Lin Townsend returned, he carefully lowered the

plates, and it was then she noticed his slight tremble. Her plate wobbled just as he let go, and it clattered onto the counter. Lin winced and closed his eyes.

A sliver of fear cut through Yvette's heart, but she remained silent while he took the stool next to her.

Lin picked up his cup of coffee, and this time his hand was steady. After he took a sip, he set it back down and turned to Yvette. "Go on. Say it."

"I wasn't going to say anything." She forked a piece of pie and shoved it in her mouth.

Her dad shook his head. "You never were a very good liar."

Yvette swallowed her pie and turned to look at her dad. "When did the tremors start?"

"It isn't a tremor." He held his hand out to prove his statement. "It's just because I've been working more hours than usual since Clay's been gone on his honeymoon, and I'm possibly overdoing it a bit."

"Oh. I guess I thought your strength was improving," she said quietly. "You look so much like your old self." She did her best to keep the emotion that was seizing her insides from showing on her face.

But she obviously failed, because her dad covered her hands with his and squeezed. "I just need to give it time. Don't worry, Rusty. Your old dad isn't going anywhere. I still have plenty of living to do."

Tears stung the backs of her eyes and she silently cursed herself for being too emotional. She just couldn't help it. The tears started rolling silently down her cheeks.

"Come here." He draped his arm around her shoulders and pulled her in for a sideways hug.

She gladly wrapped her arms around him and rested her head on his shoulder. Even though he was thinner, he was still solid, and his hug made her feel just as safe as it had when she'd been a little girl. She sniffed back her tears and said, "I know Clay's out of town and you love the brewery, but—"

"I know what you're going to say," he said, still holding her against his shoulder. "But I'm taking care of myself. Just half days to watch over the brewing process and keep up with paperwork. Rhys is stepping up and doing a great job. The truth is, we could hand everything over to him if it wasn't for the fact that I'm going stir crazy at home."

She glanced up at him. "I assume your doctor said it's okay?"

He laughed. "Yes, Yvette. I'm all cleared. Want to see my doctor's note?"

"Yes." She smiled up at him and dabbed her eyes with her napkin.

"Of course you do." He kissed the top of her head and released her. "Too bad the dog ate it."

"Which one? Buffy or Xena?" She was betting Xena, her sister Faith's puppy who her sister described as the devil in shih tzu's clothing.

"I'm not ratting anyone out." His eyes crinkled at the corners in bemusement as he took a bite of pie. After he washed it down with a sip of coffee, he said, "Enough about me. Want to tell me what's driving you to drink so early in the morning?"

She sighed. "I think I've made a huge mistake."

"How big is huge?" he asked as he put the fork down and gave her his full attention.

"Life altering." Her stomach pitched as she thought of Jacob Burton and the fact that she now had to share her store with a perfect stranger. *Well, not so much a stranger anymore,* she thought. She stifled a groan and silently cursed Isaac. Nothing about what had happened in the last few months was fair. Isaac had already moved into a fancy house across town with his accountant, and now also he had a nice sum of cash. What did she have? Her highly leveraged home and half her business.

"*You* made the mistake?" he asked surprised. "That's impossible. The Yvette I know is far too careful."

"If only I had been this time, Dad," she said sullenly into her beer. "My new business partner, Jacob Burton, isn't going to work out. He's not… well, let's just say he isn't at all what I expected."

He frowned. "What does that mean?"

"He's trying to take over the store and make big changes without even talking to me about it. It's *my* store. Can you believe it? He's acting like he's CEO and I'm just one of his underlings. I won't let that happen. No man is going to pull the rug out from under me again. I won't stand for it."

Her dad's face darkened, and his frown turned to a scowl. "He's only been there ten minutes. How could he possibly know what changes your store needs?"

She gave him a tiny smile, her heart swelling with love, knowing that no matter what, her father was always on her side. "That's pretty much what I said." Yvette filled him in on the café plans and how Jacob had already ordered supplies. "There's also an entire action plan with a calendar in place, none of which he talked to me about."

The irritation on her father's face vanished. "A café? What would it serve?"

"Dad!" Yvette stared at him with her mouth open. "You aren't on his side, are you? We can't compete with Incantation Café. That's just wrong."

"Of course I'm not on his side, sweetheart. I've always got my girls' backs. Your new business partner definitely should have spoken to you first. No doubt about it, but I was just thinking that a café in the bookstore isn't a bad idea—"

"I will not take business away from the Pelshes." Her

eyebrows pinched together as she stared at her father in confusion. "Dad, how could you even suggest such a thing?"

"What if it wasn't competition?" He waved a hand at the coffee mug sitting in front of him. "You are aware we get our coffee beans from Incantation Café, right?"

"Of course I am, but you're not serving lattes and pastries."

He laughed. "What do you think the pie is? And the only reason we don't serve lattes and other fancy coffee drinks is because our customers don't request them. But if they did, I'd work something out with Mary."

Mary Pelsh and her husband owned Incantation Café. They were good friends of the Townsend family, which was just one of the reasons Yvette had been so adamant about not competing with them. But her dad's words made her reconsider. "So you're thinking something more like a partnership, rather than competing for the same customers."

"Exactly." He shrugged one shoulder. "The more cups of coffee we sell here at the brewery, the better it is for Incantation's bottom line."

She nodded. He had a solid point. In fact, she loved the idea and couldn't wait to go talk to Mary about the possibilities. The only problem was that now she was going to have to eat crow where Jacob was concerned. *Dammit.* He'd think he'd won that round. Still, if they were going to give a bookstore café a try, they were going to do it on her terms.

"Thanks, Dad," she said and pushed her empty pie plate away. "As usual, your advice is spot on."

"You're welcome." He cast her an appraising glance. "Does this mean you aren't going to cut Jacob Burton loose just yet?"

Now that she saw a way around her biggest objection, she had to admit that his café idea wasn't a terrible one. And he certainly did understand the book business. But if he tried to steamroll right over her again, things were going to get ugly fast. "Maybe not just yet. We'll definitely need to work out some ground rules, though."

"That's true of every great relationship, love," he said and patted her hand.

Yvette let out a sardonic laugh. "Is that why you and Clair still live in separate houses after fifteen years together?" Clair was his longtime girlfriend. For most of their relationship they only saw each other about twice a week, but since her father had been diagnosed with cancer, Clair had been around more often.

"Yep." He finished off the rest of his coffee then slid off the stool. "Are you still coming by for dinner tonight? Faith and Noel will be there. Clair's cooking lasagna."

"I wouldn't miss it," Yvette said, hoping that one day when she was ready to date again, she wouldn't end up with a part time relationship like her father's. While she cherished her store, she actually had loved being married and had been thinking that it might even be time to start a family. Too bad her husband had turned out to be in love with another man.

Her father held his arms open. "Give your old man a hug before I go back to work."

Yvette let her dad wrap her in his safe embrace. Once again, she was reminded of how thin he'd gotten, and when she pulled away, she said, "You need more pie."

His lips twitched. "How much?"

"With every meal. That's an order. Got it?"

"Got it." He kissed the top of her head, and as he strolled back to his office he called over to Rhys, "Did you hear that? Pie for every meal from here on out."

"What kind?" Rhys asked without missing a beat.

"Blackberry. If we're out, then apple."

"I'm on it." Rhys made a note on his chart, nodded to Yvette, and then crossed the bar to flip the open sign. The brewery was officially open, and that meant her pity party was over. Time to get back to the store.

Yvette, feeling a thousand times better than she had when she'd barged into the brewery, reached into her bag to grab her wallet. None of the Townsend girls paid for drinks or meals at their father's brewery, but without fail, each of them left generous tips for the staff. As teenagers, they'd all worked there at one time or another and felt a kinship with all the servers. She threw a couple bills on the bar and headed out.

CHAPTER 4

Yvette swept into the Incantation Café, ready to take on the world. The more she thought about partnering with Mary, the more excited she became. She stood just inside, rubbing her cold hands together, waiting for the warmth to thaw her frozen nose. It was early January, and Keating Hollow sat about thirty miles inland from the northern California coast. The air was damp and had chilled her to the bone.

"Hey, Yvette!" Hanna, the Pelshes' daughter, waved from her place behind the counter. Her dark skin glowed under the recessed lights, and her wide, welcoming smile made Yvette grin back at her.

"Hey, Hanna." Yvette strode past the mismatched tables and chairs to meet Hanna at the register. "Is your mom in today?"

"Sure. She's in the back doing paperwork. Want me to get her?"

"Yes, please, but can I get a coffee first? A big one." After the two ill-advised beers, Yvette needed the caffeine to perk herself up.

"Of course." Hanna filled a large cup of coffee, handed it to Yvette, and waved off her attempts to pay for it. "Next time." Then she disappeared into the back.

Yvette doctored her coffee with a healthy dose of cream and took a long sip. She was still standing near the counter waiting for Mary when she heard the door open, followed by the sound of her husband's voice.

Ex-husband, she reminded herself.

He was chattering about his gym workout and how hard he'd been working.

"Well, babe, your abs certainly look like it," another man said.

Yvette jerked her head and laid eyes on the prettiest man she'd ever seen. He had bronze skin, brilliant blue eyes, and a body that looked like it was made for a Calvin Klein ad. Red-hot anger shot through her as she stared at Jake Jackson, the love of Isaac's life and the man who'd ultimately broken up her marriage. In a moment of weakness, she'd decided that if Isaac could have a Jake, then she could too. It wasn't long after that when she'd left the wedding party with Jacob.

Isaac's face lit up with a pleased smile as he slipped his hand into Jake's. Happiness radiated off them, and for the second time that day, Yvette wished with everything she had that the earth would open up and swallow her whole.

"Yvette?" Isaac asked, surprise coloring his tone.

She had no idea why he was so surprised. It wasn't as if she never frequented the café. It was less than a mile from her store. "Isaac," she said coolly. "How are you?"

He quickly dropped Jake's hand as his cheeks turned bright pink. "Fine." He turned to Jake and whispered something then strode over to Yvette and took her by the arm, leading her toward a table near the window. "What exactly do you think you're doing?"

She froze and yanked her arm from him. "What do you mean, 'what do I think I'm doing?' Getting coffee. What does it look like I'm doing?"

He frowned and shook his head. "I'm talking about Saturday night. Everyone saw you leave with that bartender."

"So? It's nobody's business what I do, especially not yours." Yvette cut her gaze to Jake, made a face, and then turned her attention back to Isaac. "You served me with divorce papers, remember?"

"This isn't about me," he said, his cheeks now turning dark red. "It's about… well, Yvette, you didn't even know that guy. And from what I hear, you took him home with you. What's going on? That isn't you. You take your time and are careful with relationships."

"It's none of your business, Isaac," she said coolly. "Or did you forget that you gave up that right a few weeks ago when you decided you were in love with someone else?"

He sighed heavily. "Just because I finally stopped lying to myself doesn't mean I don't love you, Vette. You were my best friend. I just want what's best for you. We both know rushing into any sort of physical relationship isn't your style. You care too deeply and always have. I'm just asking you to be careful. I don't want to see you hurt anymore."

Intense anger rose up the back of her throat like bile, and Yvette wondered if she opened her mouth if she'd start to breathe fire. For half a second, she contemplated ripping the top off her coffee cup and dumping the contents over his head. How dare he act concerned and question anything she chose to do? "Your opinion on this subject isn't welcome, Isaac. I think we're done here."

She turned and started to walk back to the counter, but Isaac reached out and grabbed her wrist. "Yvette, wait."

Everything inside of her tensed as she glanced back at him. "Let go. Now."

They both stared at his hand wrapped around her arm. It wasn't until someone cleared their throat that he let go.

"Is everything okay here?" the new arrival asked.

Oh, goddess above, Yvette thought as she tilted her head and stared at the ceiling. This was not happening right now. It couldn't be. Why had Jacob Burton chosen that particular moment to patronize the coffee shop?

"My *wife* and I are just fine," Isaac said.

"Wife?" he asked casually as he glanced at Isaac's boyfriend. "I was under the impression that she was divorced."

"She's not divorced yet," Isaac said, his eyes blazing.

Yvette stared at Isaac, her eyes wide as shock rolled through her. He was angry and… jealous. Her shock turned to pure satisfaction, and she took a step closer to Jacob out of sheer spite. She glanced at Jacob. "The paperwork has already been filed. We're just waiting for it to be finalized."

He nodded and placed his hand on the small of her back as he turned his attention back to Isaac. "Looks like she's free to fraternize with whomever she pleases then."

Isaac glared at Jacob. "And you think you're just the guy for the job, do you?"

"This is ridiculous." The other Jake stood up abruptly, knocking his chair over in the process. "Isaac what is wrong with you?" he asked in a disgusted tone. Then without waiting for an answer, he swept out of the café.

"Jake, wait!" Isaac called out as he took off after his significant other. Just as he reached for the door handle, he glanced over his shoulder at Yvette. "I was just trying to look out for you."

"Maybe you should've thought about that before you left

her and forced her to buy you out of her bookstore," Jacob said calmly.

"That is none of your business," Isaac said.

"Actually," Yvette said, "it is. He's my new business partner." She raised her eyebrows and nodded toward the plate-glass window where they could all see Isaac's boyfriend pacing back and forth on the sidewalk. He had his hands fisted in his hair, and he appeared to be talking to himself. "It looks like you have more pressing problems to deal with than my personal life."

Jacob's body trembled with a silent chuckle, and she smiled up at him.

"Dammit, Yvette," Isaac said. Then he yanked the door open and hurried outside.

Yvette and Jacob watched Isaac chase after his significant other as Jake stalked down the street, shaking his head.

"That was entertaining," Yvette said, grinning up at Jacob. "Thanks for... well, you know. Having my back."

He smiled down at her. "Any time. That guy has some nerve."

She snorted. "He does, doesn't he?"

Jacob just nodded.

The two of them fell silent, and suddenly Yvette became acutely aware of his hand still resting on the small of her back. His touch seemed to burn straight through her shirt and into her skin. She quickly sidestepped away from him and cleared her throat. "Sorry. I just—"

"It's fine, Yvette." He held out his hand. "Why don't we start over? Hello, I'm Jacob Burton, your new business partner."

The tension drained from her shoulders, and she nodded as she gripped and shook his hand. "Yvette Townsend. It's nice to meet you. And for the record, I'm sorry I blew up at you this morning."

"Don't be," he said, shaking his head. "You were right. I shouldn't have steamrolled you with my ideas."

"True. You shouldn't have. But… after giving it some thought, I think you might be on to something. Customers would like a coffee bar. And that's why I'm here." She turned and spotted Mary and Hanna watching them from behind the counter. Yvette waved at them.

They grinned and waved back.

"I figured if we partnered with the café, it would be a win-win for both businesses. Care to join me while I have a chat with Mary over there?"

"A partnership," he said, nodding. "I like it. Lead on, Ms. Townsend. Lead on."

"This way." Yvette strode over to the counter where Mary was waiting for her. She gave the other woman a hug. When she released her, she said, "Mary Pelsh, meet Jacob Burton, the new co-owner of Hollow Books."

"Hi." The older woman held her hand out and smiled at him. "You're a handsome one."

Jacob chuckled and took her hand. "Thank you. You're not bad yourself. Love the hair."

She used her free hand to very gently pat her dark curls and glanced away as she said, "You're too kind."

"It's very nice to meet you, Mary," Jacob said. "I hope we're not interrupting you."

"Oh no, not at all." She glanced down at their still-clasped hands then let out a small gasp. "Wow. You're quite a gifted air witch, aren't you?"

"An air witch, sure. Gifted?" He shrugged one shoulder. "The fact that you can tell what kind of a witch I am just by shaking my hand tells me that you're the gifted one."

Mary cut her gaze to Yvette and lowered her voice as she said, "He's charming, too."

"Yes, he is," Yvette agreed. "The customers will love him."

"They sure will," Hanna cut in, pumping her eyebrows. "So... are you single?"

"Hanna!" Yvette said.

Jacob pulled his hand out of Mary's and shoved them both in his front pockets. "I'm single, but..." He glanced at Yvette quickly, before turning his charm on Hanna and adding, "I'm not really in the market to date right now, so don't go trying to set me up with all your girlfriends." He paused then added, "At least not yet."

His words irritated Yvette, and she had to stifle a frown. He just said he wasn't in the market to date, but he sure hadn't had any problems jumping into bed with her. But then, she hadn't intended to date him either. That had been a one-time thing.

Dammit. Isaac was right. She wasn't one for casual relationships. Her reaction to Jacob proved it. She closed her eyes and sucked in a fortifying breath. She had to let the other night go. It was the only way she was going to be able to work with Jacob.

"Mary," Yvette said, making eye contact with the other woman. "We were hoping we could talk to you about stocking the bookstore with your coffee and maybe some specialty items. Do you have time to sit down and discuss some ideas?"

"Sure," Mary said. "Come on back to my office."

Mary's office was small but neat. A wooden desk sat at one end of the room, and a white plastic table full of stacked merchandise sat at the other. Mary pulled two folding metal chairs out of a closet and set them up for Yvette and Jacob before taking a seat behind her desk.

Yvette perched on the edge of her chair and leaned forward, while Jacob sat back with one ankle propped on his opposite knee.

"So," Mary said as she flipped open a notebook. "What were you thinking? Coffee beans? Pastries? Cookies?"

"Yes, but not the regular stuff you serve here," Yvette said.

Jacob turned and gave her a questioning glance. She gave him a self-satisfied smile.

Mary tilted her head to the side. "Specialty items?"

"Yes." Yvette nodded. "Of course the coffee will be your regular blends, unless you have something else you recommend, but for pastries I was thinking it would be fun if we could get themed cupcakes that are decorated with nods to popular books, cookies with famous literary quotes, and maybe slices of cake that have edges that look like book spines." She turned to Jacob. "What do you think?"

His eyes crinkled at the corners as he flashed her a smile. "It's brilliant, Yvette. Much better than anything I was thinking."

Yvette's insides warmed, and she started to feel as if this partnership might actually be for the best. She turned back to Mary who was frantically scribbling in her notebook.

"'It was a dark and stormy night,'" Mary said to herself. She glanced up and continued, "'Frankly, my dear, I don't give a damn.' 'The boy who lived.'"

Yvette grinned, recognizing all three lines instantly. "Nice. *Paul Clifford, Gone with the Wind,* and *Harry Potter*. How about 'Ye are Blood of my Blood, and Bone of my Bone?'"

"*Outlander!* Yes," Mary said, bouncing in her seat. She scribbled it down, then stared pointedly at Jacob. "How about you? Any lines you want to see on the cookies?"

Jacob shifted in his seat. "Um…"

After he squirmed for a minute, Yvette laughed. "Seriously? Mr. Bayside Books can't come up with one quote?"

"I can, I just…" He gritted his teeth.

"Don't worry, Mary. I'll get you a list," Yvette said.

"Wait. I have one," Jacob said. "'Nothing is so painful to the human mind as a great and sudden change.'"

Yvette gave him an appraising look and nodded. "Nice one."

"What's it from?" Mary asked.

"*Frankenstein*," Jacob said and sat back in his chair.

"Perfect." Mary scribbled a couple more notes. When she was done she said, "I love it. I assume you'll want fresh stock every day?"

"Yes. That's the plan. We'll place conservative orders to start, but if they take off, we hope to be a bulk account," Yvette said.

Mary waved an unconcerned hand. "Don't you worry about that. Whatever you order will be as a wholesale customer. I'm always thrilled to partner with other Keating Hollow businesses."

Her dad had been spot-on with his advice. She'd need to remember to thank him, preferably with one of Mary's coffee cakes.

"Give me a few days," Mary said, "and I'll get some samples over to you. Then if you like what you see, we can work out a contract."

"Perfect," Yvette said as she stood.

Jacob got to his feet and offered Mary his hand again. "I look forward to tasting whatever you come up with," he said as he shook her hand.

"You bet your sweet cheeks you are," she said with a wink. "My cupcakes will make you fall in love with me."

He laughed. "I bet."

"That's enough," Yvette said, pulling Jacob from the office before Mary had a chance to drool on him. "We have a bookstore to run. Mary, call me when you have something ready for us."

"Oh, I will," she called. "Sooner rather than later!"

"Is she always that excited?" Jacob asked her as they made their way back into the café's storefront.

Yvette shook her head. "Nope. Only when handsome new residents flirt with her."

"I wasn't flirting," he protested.

"Sure." She patted his arm. "You just keep telling yourself that."

CHAPTER 5

Jacob Burton followed Yvette back into the bookstore. When he'd left over an hour ago to get a cup coffee, he'd been frustrated by his new situation. Now he was amused. He'd enjoyed teaming up with her to put her ex in his place. The guy had been way out of line, acting as if he had some say over Yvette's decisions. And Jacob had been more than happy to help her put him in his place.

Of course as soon as the jackhole had hightailed it out of the café, things had gotten a little uncomfortable. But that was only because the chemistry between him and Yvette was off the charts. Touching her had made him want her all over again. Then there was her sass. There was nothing he liked better than a woman who wasn't afraid to stand up for herself.

Smart, sexy, and independent. Those were Jacob's three weaknesses, and Yvette had them in spades. He was doomed. He slowed his steps, putting more distance between them. He needed to cool it, stop thinking about her as the woman he took home the other night, and put her strictly in the business zone. Because he well knew that romance in the business place was a recipe for disaster.

She paused at her office door. "We should probably sit down and discuss the other ideas in your folder."

Surprise rendered him speechless for a moment. Sure, she'd come around on the café idea, but he hadn't expected her to be so willing to consider more changes so soon.

"You don't have to look so surprised. I'm not completely unreasonable," she said with a teasing smile.

"I'm just…" He shook his head. "It's been a surprising day."

"You can say that again." Her long chestnut hair swung to the side as she turned and disappeared into her office.

He followed, trying and failing to keep his eyes off her backside. If only she hadn't filled out her jeans so well, then he might not have missed whatever it was she was saying.

"How about right here?" she waved an arm at the space under the window.

"Pardon?" he asked.

"For your desk," she said. "We could put it here until we can get the storage area cleaned out and set up as a proper office. It currently doesn't have a window in there, but it shouldn't be too hard to put one in."

"Oh, right." Sharing an office with this lovely creature wasn't going to bode well for his productivity. He was going to need to get his own space set up as soon as possible.

She cleared her throat. "I'm sorry. There isn't much other choice, unless you just want to set up every day where the new café is going to go."

He frowned. "Why would I want to do that? Here is fine."

She let out a long breath, looking relieved. "Okay, good. I thought for a moment you were unhappy with the situation."

He shook his head and moved over to help her clear the

space. "Do you have another desk around here, or do I need to pick one up?"

She bit her lower lip. "It's buried in the storage room."

"Of course it is," he said with a chuckle. "Well, shall we go rescue it?"

Yvette glanced at her desk and the pile of invoices waiting for her. "Absolutely. Anything to save me from catching up on the payables."

Jacob followed her gaze to the stack of invoices and suppressed a groan. He'd already had a look at the books and wasn't expecting any expenses until the end of the month. If she was just paying more invoices now, that meant their hopes of having positive cash flow for the month just flew out the window.

"Don't look like that," she said, slapping his arm. "It's not that bad. They're just the invoices from the last-minute December orders. We still had a good holiday season."

Good was the problem, he thought. What they needed was *great*. "How good is good?"

Yvette rolled her eyes. "You've been here less than one day. Can't you just settle in before we go to war over the books?"

No. The word flashed in his mind like a neon sign. Every instinct told him to stay right where they were and to go over the financials with a fine-toothed comb, but he knew if he suggested such a thing at the moment, then their tenuous truce would turn back into a war. "You're right. Let's get set up. We can talk about the budget and projections later."

"Sure," she said, but her tone was less than enthusiastic.

"Numbers aren't your thing?" he asked.

"Is it terrible if I say no?" she asked with a grimace. "Isaac used to do the books for me. He'd keep me up to speed, so I always knew what was going on, but I have to admit, it's not my favorite part of the business."

"Then it appears we're a match made in heaven, Ms. Townsend. Because numbers happen to be one of the few things I'm very good at. I don't mind taking on that role," he said as he followed her into a dark room at the end of the hallway.

She flipped the light on and suddenly tensed as she glanced around.

Jacob's eyes went wide as he took in the pyramid of boxes. "Is this *all* back inventory?"

"Uh… yes?" she said, as if she were unsure of herself.

"Son of a—" His phone started playing "Forget You," the R-rated version. He grabbed it, silenced the ringer, and stared at Sienna's face flashing on his screen. She was the last person he wanted to talk to right then… the last person he wanted to talk to ever, for that matter, but they still had unsettled business. "Sorry. I have to take this."

Yvette nodded.

He turned, already striding out of the storage room as he quickly answered the call. "Do you have paperwork for me?" he asked by way of greeting.

"What, no happy New Year or how was your Christmas?" she asked, her voice silky and smooth.

"Honestly, Sienna, we both know you don't care what I did over the holidays, and I know I certainly don't want to hear about your Caribbean vacation." He reached the front door of the store and strode out into the cold.

"So your dad *did* tell you then," she said. "Bri and I—"

Jacob cleared his throat as pure anger made his throat raw. What planet was she living on that made her think he had any interest in hearing about the vacation his ex-fiancée had taken with his ex-best friend? "Just get to the point, Sienna. Tell me why you called. Is it something to do with Enchanted Bliss?"

"Why do you always have to be in such a hurry to talk business?" she asked with a whine in her tone.

Jacob paced the sidewalk. "Maybe because there isn't anything else to discuss."

"You know that isn't true, Jacob. We had a business together. We almost got married. And—"

"And you turned the daily operations over to a teenager who had no idea how to run the place while you were off sleeping with my best friend. Meanwhile, I went back to work for my father just so we could get your dream beach house you were so desperate to buy." The familiar fury washed over him, and he had an intense desire to smash his phone on the sidewalk.

The anger that had consumed him for the last year was the main reason he'd escaped Los Angeles for Keating Hollow in the first place. And it had mostly worked for the five days that he'd been there. He hadn't thought of Sienna or Brian hardly at all since he'd rolled into town and not once since he'd laid eyes on Yvette.

"Jacob," she said with a sigh. "I'm just calling because the realtor has closing paperwork for you to sign on the house. And while you're here, we might as well finish the deal for Enchanted Bliss."

"We can do everything by email," he said coolly. "I'll have my lawyer get in touch." Then before she could say anything else, he ended the call. His phone immediately started ringing again, but he silenced it. He knew her too well. All she wanted was his attention. But this time he'd be damned if she was going to get it.

Jacob ignored the third phone call from Sienna and immediately called Norm, the family lawyer.

"Stanley, Stanley, and Cooper," Penny, Norm's assistant, said into the phone.

"Hey, Pen. It's Jacob. I need to talk to Norm. Is he around?"

"Sure is, doll," she said, sounding like an old Hollywood siren from the 1950s. "Hold on for a quick sec."

There was a click on the line, followed by another, then Norm said, "Jacob, I was just about to get in touch with you. Ms. Teller's lawyer finally sent over the paperwork for Enchanted Bliss. There's been a development."

His stomach churned, making him nauseated. "What development?"

"Ms. Teller is refusing to sign the final paperwork unless you're here in person. That includes the sale of the beach house, too."

"This is a joke, right?" He couldn't imagine any valid reason why Sienna would need to see him, unless it was just to feed her own ego or try to create some new narrative that didn't paint her as the cheating gold digger she'd turned out to be.

"I'm afraid not. Her lawyer said she's just flat out refusing until she sees you in person."

He held back a curse. "When do I need to be there?"

"Saturday. Ms. Teller is insisting it's the only day she has free. If you're agreeable, I can make arrangements to be available. And if we're lucky, you can fly in first thing. I'll set up the appointments back to back, and you can get out of town on an evening flight."

Saturday, Jacob thought as he rolled his eyes. Why did she have to insist on making the lawyers work on the weekend? She was a piece of work.

As much as he appreciated his lawyer trying to reassure him he wouldn't need to spend much time in Los Angeles, he knew better. He'd bet his last fifty bucks he wouldn't make it out of town until at least Monday. If Sienna was insisting on seeing him, she wanted something. And she wasn't going to sign anything until she got it. Still, if he wanted to be free of her, he really didn't have any choice but to show up. "I'll be there. Just email me the times of the meetings and I'll work around them."

"All right. I'll have Penny set it up. See you Saturday."

He ended the call. It immediately started vibrating. Sienna was still trying to get in touch with him. Disgusted, he ignored her and shoved the phone in his pocket. Instead of going back into the shop, he took off down the street, walking at a brisk pace. He needed to work off some steam before going back into the bookstore. He didn't want to inadvertently take out his frustration on anyone else, especially Yvette.

CHAPTER 6

Yvette stood in the storage room staring at the boxes. There was far more extra inventory in there than normal. Something was seriously off. She strode quickly back to her office and rummaged through the invoices still sitting on her desk. All of them were what she expected except for the one on the bottom. She let the others fall to the desk as her eyes bugged out.

"Oh no." She closed her eyes and shook her head as if she'd read it incorrectly and needed a fresh look. But when she scanned it again, there was no mistaking her error. Instead of ordering ten copies each of the four-book series, she'd inadvertently ordered ten *cases* of each. And because they were published by a small independent publisher, they were non-returnable.

A pit formed in her gut. How had she let this happen? In all the years she'd owned the bookstore, they'd never made such an erroneous error. Isaac had done most of the ordering as well as the bookkeeping. It wasn't that she didn't know how, it was just the way they'd divided the tasks that needed to be done. She glanced at the invoice, hoping she could blame the error on Isaac. But when she saw the date the order had been placed, that fantasy flew out the window. This order had been made the week after Isaac had moved out and had abruptly stopped helping her at the bookstore.

No wonder she'd messed up. Not only had she not been completely familiar with the ordering software, she'd also been a complete emotional mess. She slammed her fist down on the desk in pure frustration. Why couldn't she have uncovered this error last month, before she had a partner to answer to? She sank down on the desk and buried her face in her hands. Good goddess, Jacob was going to think she was an idiot. And he'd be right.

She sat down in her office chair, turned on her computer, and meticulously went through each and every invoice. Once they were all logged and paid, she looked at the bank balance and winced. It was lower than was comfortable. No wonder Jacob had been concerned.

Yvette sat back, her face flushed and warm with her humiliation. She had to do something to fix this. But how? Even though she knew the answer would be no, she picked up the phone, called the supplier, and asked if there was any way she could make a return. The answer was a solid no. It was what she'd been expecting, so instead of getting upset, she started to brainstorm a plan B.

First things first. She needed to get eyes on those extra books. Nothing was going to happen with them sitting in the storage room.

After spending the rest of the day unpacking boxes and then working on the front window display, Yvette was sweaty and half-starved as she stood outside her shop, eyeing the front window. She had to admit, it looked good. Really good. But compared to the other front windows on Main Street in the enchanted town, it wasn't quite enough to wow the tourists. It needed something… something magic. What she needed was an air witch. She doubted Brinn had the skill to make it as elaborate as Yvette envisioned, and she was busy closing up the store. Yvette decided she'd worry about it in the morning.

She pulled her phone out of her pocket and glanced at the time. It was almost six, and Jacob was still MIA. Truth be told, since she'd realized her error, she hadn't exactly been looking forward to his return. She'd wanted to have a solid plan in place before she had to fess up to her error. And while the window was a good start, she still needed to figure out some sort of event to bring customers in.

Still, she was a little worried about him. He'd left hours ago to take his call and had just disappeared. Biting her lower lip, she pulled up his contact number and hit call. It rang three times before going straight to voicemail. "Jacob, it's Yvette. I'm just calling to… well, I guess just to make sure you're okay. You left abruptly today, and I wanted to make sure you didn't get lost or something. If you get this, just do me a favor and check in to put my mind at ease. Thanks."

She ended the call and felt like a fool. Jacob was a grown man. He certainly didn't need her acting like a mother hen. It wasn't as if he had regular hours he was supposed to be working the store. He was part owner, not a sales clerk. She strode back into the store and made a beeline for her office. After picking up her purse and her keys, she strolled back out into the store.

"Brinn?" she called out.

Her employee stepped out from behind the register counter. "Yeah?"

"I'm headed out for the night. Do you need anything before I go?"

Brinn shook her head, her blond ponytail swaying gracefully behind her. "I've got it. Have a good evening."

"You, too."

YVETTE STEERED her Ford Mustang down the mile-long drive that led to her father's house. The familiar twinkle lights lining the trees made her smile, and the day's tension started to slip away. She always felt whole when she was around her family, like she was exactly where she was supposed to be.

Cars were already lined up in her dad's drive. She parked behind Noel's old SUV and hopped out. Before she could even make it to the front porch, the door flew open and a small brindle colored shih tzu darted out, followed by Yvette's six-year-old niece Daisy. Her dark curls were just as wild as she was as she chased the puppy into the yard, yelling, "Buffy! Buffy, come back!"

Yvette's sister Noel stepped out onto the porch, glanced at her daughter and the puppy running in circles, then smiled at Yvette. "I see you managed to survive the day. Can the same be said for your smokin' hot business partner?"

"Hot business partner?" Drew asked as he appeared from the house. "Has my girl set her sights on some new guy in town?"

Noel rolled her eyes and slipped her arm around his waist. "Like I have time to deal with one more man in my life."

They both turned their attention to Yvette. Noel raised her eyebrows in question. "Well, how did the rest of the day go?"

"We came to terms on the café. We've decided to partner with Mary and the Incantation Café. But besides that?" Yvette shrugged "No idea. He got a phone call and left. I haven't seen him since before lunch."

"I saw him at the brewery," Drew offered. "Said hello, but that's about it."

"At least he didn't drown in the river," Yvette muttered.

"What?" Noel asked with a chuckle. "Why would you think that?"

"No reason. Come on, let's get inside. I'm starving."

"Daisy," Noel called. "Time for dinner."

The little girl gave her mother a half-hearted, "Okay." But she continued to chase Buffy, and Yvette knew Daisy wouldn't be obeying her mother's instructions without a little help.

"Daisy, aren't you going to give your aunt a hug?" Yvette asked, walking over to her and the puppy.

Her niece immediately made a beeline to her aunt, her arms wide. Yvette crouched down and was nearly knocked over when Daisy barreled into her and hung on tight as Yvette lifted her up and swung her around. "I missed you, sweet girl," Yvette whispered in her ear.

"I missed you, too, Auntie." Daisy planted a loud kiss on Yvette's cheek and then giggled as Yvette twirled her some more.

"Auntie's hungry," Yvette said, already walking up to the door. "Wanna come in so we can get some dinner?"

Daisy nodded enthusiastically, but before they could make their grand entrance, the little girl shouted, "Drew, get Buffy!"

"Yes, princess," he said with a laugh and strode over to collect the dog.

"She has him wrapped around her little finger," Noel said, not bothering to lower her voice.

"And I wouldn't have it any other way," Drew said, winking at her.

Noel fingered the sapphire promise ring hanging around her neck and got a dopey look on her face.

A trace of jealousy rolled through Yvette, but she ignored it and smiled at her sister, focusing on the fact that she truly was happy that Noel had found someone who loved her and Daisy so much. It was just hard to watch a new relationship blossom when your own had blown up so spectacularly.

The house was warm and full of laughter as they entered the living room. Olive, Clay's daughter and Abby's new step daughter, sat with Yvette's youngest sister Faith in front of a crackling fire. Olive was staying with Noel and Daisy while Clay and Abby were on their honeymoon. The pair were playing cards, while Lin and Clair milled around in the kitchen, putting the finishing touches on dinner.

Yvette glanced at the table that was already set and frowned. "Why nine place settings?" She quickly counted the heads in the room, making sure she hadn't missed anyone. Six adults and two children. "Is someone else joining us for dinner?"

"Dad!" Noel called out. "You didn't tell her? I thought you said you were going to call and let her know."

"I got busy," he called back as he pulled something that looked a lot like garlic bread from the oven. He placed it on the stove and turned around. "Does it really matter? It's just dinner."

Dread crawled up the back of Yvette's throat and threatened to choke her. She gripped the back of the couch and forced out, "Please tell me he didn't invite Isaac. Because I already had one run-in with him today. It did *not* go well."

"You did?" Noel asked, her eyes going wide with curiosity. "What happened?"

Her righteous indignation came roaring back with a

vengeance. "Can you believe he had the nerve to lecture me about..." She lowered her voice and whispered, "about leaving Abby's wedding with Jacob?"

"You're kidding me!" Noel said, placing her hands on her hips. "After how he left your marriage, I can't believe he went there. What was his problem with it? Did he think you were tarnishing your reputation or something?" Her expression turned from surprised to disgusted. "For a gay man, he's surprisingly old-fashioned."

"Judgmental is the word you're looking for," Yvette said as she took a seat on the stool at the counter and nodded her thanks to Clair when the other woman passed her a glass of red wine.

"Jackass might be closer," Clair interjected, making both Yvette and Noel laugh.

"That, too," Yvette agreed. "But to answer your question, no. He didn't imply I'd be a sullied woman or anything. He basically said I was too emotional for casual relationships and that he was worried about me."

"Ahh," Noel said, nodding, making a strand of her long blond hair fall over one eye. She pushed it back. "I can see that."

"See what?" Yvette took a sip of her wine. "That I'm too emotional or that he'd be worried about me."

"Both." Noel sat next to her and placed her hand over Yvette's. "Listen, you have every reason to hate Isaac. He blew up your life. Not only did you lose a marriage, you almost lost your store. So I get it. And if you want to build voodoo dolls and stick pins where the sun doesn't shine, I'll be there with bells on."

Yvette let out a small chuckle. "You would probably sew the dolls yourself."

"I am crafty," she said with a nod. "Anyway, Dad didn't invite Isaac for family dinner. He isn't *that* clueless."

"Then who?" Yvette said just as the doorbell rang.

Daisy darted into the entryway, and a second later Yvette heard the door open, followed by a very familiar male voice.

Yvette turned and stared at Noel. "*Jacob* is here?"

She raised her hands and half-heartedly waved her fingers. "Surprise."

"Who invited him?" Her heart sped up as her nerves took over. So much for having a nice relaxing evening with her family.

Noel pointed at their father.

Whipping around, Yvette glared at Lin. "*Dad*! What are you doing to me?"

"Nothing, Rusty. I just thought it was a good idea for the family to get to know your new business partner, that's all." He gave Yvette a pat on the arm as he passed her and held his hand out to the man in question. "Jacob, I'm glad you could make it."

"Wouldn't miss it for the world, Mr. Townsend. Thanks for inviting me. Home cooked meals are a rarity for me these days."

"Thank Clair, she did all the work." Lin turned and smiled at the rest of the family. "Everyone, this is Jacob Burton, the new co-owner of Hollow Books. Jacob, this is everyone." He quickly finished introducing the family, and while Jacob was saying hello to Drew, Yvette followed her father into the kitchen.

"Dad, why did you do this to me?" She'd only wanted a nice family dinner. Now she was stuck trying to act normal around Jacob. A tough act to pull off after their Saturday night antics, not to mention her error at the store she hadn't yet told him about.

"Come on, Rusty. I didn't do anything to you. I was just

being neighborly. He came by the brewery for lunch. I just happened to be helping Rhys out at the bar when he came in. Once I realized who he was, it seemed natural to invite him over." He paused and gazed down at her. "I know you two still have some kinks to work out, but is there some reason I should be hostile to him? He is Miss Maple's nephew, and he seems like a nice young man."

"No," she said, suddenly ashamed of her attitude. Embarrassed, she stared down at her hands as she added, "He is a nice man, and you were right to invite him. I should've done it myself, but... well, let's just say it was a strange day."

"I'm sure it's a tough adjustment, giving up some of the control of your store." He gave her a soft smile. "Just give it time. You'll settle into a rhythm soon enough. If not, you'll work something else out."

"Easy for you to say," she muttered as she grabbed the garlic bread and placed it on the table.

Jacob excused himself and walked over to Yvette. "I hope this is all right."

"Sure. Why wouldn't it be?" she asked with a bright smile.

He chuckled. "You know why. But I really like your dad and want to get to know the community, so when he invited me over..." Jacob raised his hands in a helpless gesture. "I had to say yes."

"It's fine, Jacob," she said, shaking her head. "We're both adults here. It's not really a surprise that dad would invite you over. He likes to get to know all the business owners in town."

"Okay then." He put his hands in his jeans pockets and rocked back on his heels. "Then I don't need to worry that this is about him being an overprotective father?"

Yvette snorted. "Please. Dad knows I can take care of myself."

"I can see that." He cleared his throat then lowered his voice as he added, “I’m sorry I took off today. I had some unfinished business to deal with, and I—”

“Jacob,” she said, raising her hand to stop him. “You don’t need to explain anything to me. You’re a co-owner, not staff. You do your thing, and I’ll do mine. As long as we’re checking in with each other, it’ll be fine.”

“Right.” He pressed his lips together into a thin line as if he was contemplating what she’d said, but before he could say anything else, Clair placed the lasagna in the middle of the table.

“Dinner’s ready,” she said. “Everyone have a seat.” She glanced at Yvette and Jacob. “You two sit at the end near Lin. He wants to get to know Keating Hollow’s newest resident.”

Of course he did. Yvette took her seat on one side of the table while Jacob sat across from her. Lin sat at the end. The rest of the family joined them, and Clair got busy dishing up the lasagna.

Everyone immediately started chattering. Olive and Daisy were at the other end of the table comparing puppy stories. Faith, who was sitting next to Jacob, interjected with a hellhound horror story of her own, then glanced over her shoulder to glare at her shih tzu that was busy trying to tear apart one of the couch cushions. She jumped up, nearly knocking over her glass of wine, and quickly secured her dog into a kennel near the far wall. The pup let out a pathetic whine and then got busy chewing on the blanket.

Faith reclaimed her seat at the table and let out an exaggerated sigh. “That dog is trying to torture me.”

“Maybe it needs obedience classes,” Jacob said.

“Ha! Obedience classes. I wish I’d thought of that,” she said sarcastically.

“Xena has failed three different puppy training courses,”

Yvette said, filling Jacob in. "We've started to call her the hell hound."

"Three?" he asked.

"Three," Lin said with a nod. "She's also eaten two arm chairs, a bedspread, three different shoes, and a power cord that was still plugged in."

"It's a miracle she didn't electrocute herself," Faith said. "You can see how the kennel is a complete necessity. I don't know how Noel ended up with the angel and I got Satan." She pointed at the sweet brindle dog curled up near Daisy. "My karma must suck."

Noel looked up from her plate and shook her head. "It's not you. Buffy had an evil streak to begin with, too. She was just a better student, I guess."

"You're probably a better trainer," Faith said. "Maybe you should take Xena."

"Oh no!" Noel held her hands up in a stop motion. "I have my hands full with Daisy, the puppy, and Drew here. Xena's all yours."

Faith shrugged. "We'll just keep working at it."

"And buying new furniture," Lin said with a scowl.

"It's your fault I even have Xena!" Faith exclaimed and went on to explain that the puppies had shown up at Lin's house one day and that's how she and Noel had both ended up with one.

The conversation remained lively through the rest of the dinner. Yvette listened to Jacob grill her father about the brewery. He wanted all the details of how it'd started, how they kept it thriving, and what his plans were for the future. He seemed genuinely interested, and Lin was all too happy to talk about the business he'd built up over the years.

Then it was Jacob's turn. Lin wanted to know all about Bayside Books, how his father got started, Jacob's role with expanding, and why he'd left recently.

Jacob got quiet for a moment as his expression went blank. Then it was as if a switch was thrown and he gave Lin a chagrined smile. "My position with Bayside Books was always meant to be temporary until a new business was on solid ground. Once it was up and running we were going to franchise. But…" He shrugged. "That partnership didn't work out, so here I am."

"You didn't want to just stay in business with your dad?" Lin asked. There wasn't any judgement in his tone, only curiosity. None of Lin's own children had shown much of an interest in running the brew pub, so Lin had hired Clay, a talented brew master. It was just luck that he and Abby had finally found their way back together. Now everyone just assumed that when the time came, Clay would run it and Lin's children would be shareholders.

"Not really. I was looking for a change," he said.

"Well, Hollow Books couldn't be more different than your dad's Bayside Books," Yvette said, raising her wine glass in a toast. "I hope you don't find it too boring here, Jacob."

His chagrined smile turned into pure amusement. "So far, boring is the last word I'd use to describe my new situation."

Yvette cleared her throat and glanced away, afraid that if she kept looking at him, she'd turn bright red and die from embarrassment. And she'd already had enough of that for one day.

Faith chuckled, but quickly covered her mouth with her fist and pretended to cough. She cleared her throat and turned to Jacob as if she hadn't just made a little scene. "I'm thinking about opening a spa here in town, and I hear you might have some experience with that."

Yvette's fingers tightened around her fork, and she had a fleeting desire to fling it at her younger sister. What was she doing? She knew that was the business he'd been talking about, the one he'd started with his ex. Yvette was one hundred percent positive that Jacob did not want to talk about either his former fiancée or the business he'd walked away from.

"Some," Jacob said stiffly. Then his tone turned to one of resentment. "My partner saw to all the details. I was just there because of my deep pockets… or so I've been told."

"Jeez," Yvette said, unable to help herself. "That's really effed up. I'm sorry, Jacob. No one deserves to be treated that way."

He took a long swig of his wine. "Turns out I should've been more discerning. My lawyer tried to talk me out of it, but I let emotions get in the way of business. It was my fault, and it won't happen again."

"It can be tough to know who to trust when you've seen so much success," Lin said with a nod. "There are times when a man needs to trust his advisors, and then there are times when he needs to trust his gut. What was your gut saying?"

Jacob stared down at his plate. When he glanced up at Lin, he said, "I think my gut got drowned out by other factors."

Lin let out a belly laugh. "I've been there, son. I've definitely been there. Next time, you'll remember."

"You'd think so, wouldn't you?" Jacob met Yvette's gaze. The two stared at each other, and a knot formed in Yvette's stomach. Judging by the regret reflected back at her, he was thinking he'd made a huge mistake the night of Abby's wedding. And even though she was certain that was probably true, she hated to admit it to herself. Hated to think that she was a *mistake*.

"Jacob," Faith said turning to him. "I understand that your last business venture was a spa. Is that correct?"

"Faith," Yvette said in a hushed whisper.

Her sister ignored her as she pressed on. "I could really use some advice, if you're willing. I've always wanted to open a high-end spa. Keating Hollow has never had one, and I'd love to change that."

Jacob cleared his throat. "Well, Sienna really was the one who—"

"Sienna was your fiancée and your partner, right?" Faith clasped her hand over her mouth. "Oh… I'm sorry," she stammered. "Forget I said anything."

Irritation flashed in Jacob's eyes. But then he blinked, and it was gone. He straightened his shoulders and when he spoke again, he was the cool and collected businessman Yvette had met early that morning. "No, need to be sorry," he told Faith. "Of course, I'd be happy to go over your business plan. Just come by the bookstore when you're ready, and I'll take a look."

"Really?" Faith's face lit up as she grinned at him. Then she placed her hand on his arm and squeezed. "You're a real gem, you know that? Is tomorrow too soon?"

"Yes," Yvette interjected, irritated on his behalf. "Give the man a week or so to settle in at the store, then you can pick his brain, okay?"

"Oh, right. Of course," she said, squeezing Jacob's arm again. "I guess I got a little excited. Sorry, didn't mean to be so pushy."

"It's all right," he said, but he glanced at Yvette and mouthed *thank you*.

She just shrugged. It wasn't as if she'd gotten him out of it; all she'd done was buy him some time.

"I'll fine tune what I already have on paper and meet up with you next week." Faith let out a nervous laugh. "Hopefully I won't look too foolish."

Jacob glanced between Faith and Yvette then chuckled softly to himself. "Something tells me that when it comes to business, the Townsend sisters rarely, if ever, look foolish."

"Well, you do have a point there," Yvette said. "There are

two things dad said we all needed to know how to do: change the oil in our cars and manage the brewery. He said if we could do that, we could do anything."

Lin laughed. "It's true isn't it? Three of you have successful businesses, and I'm sure Faith's spa will follow suit."

"I sure hope so," Faith said, twisting her napkin with both hands. "Because I'm seriously considering renting the space."

CHAPTER 7

Jacob sat at the counter with Faith Townsend and wondered how he'd ended up elbow deep in the decision making of a hypothetical spa. He couldn't care less if the massage rooms were finished with wood or stone. But if he was honest, he knew exactly why he was giving Faith Townsend his uneducated opinion on design; it was because he hadn't been able to help himself. The lure of a brand-new business, the freshness, the possibilities were all too seductive. They'd already talked about strategies, suppliers, and marketing ideas. Faith had proven to be a sponge. She wanted to know his thoughts on everything, so it wasn't a surprise when she'd asked about esthetics.

"I like both," he said. "Why not decorate the rooms differently for a range of experiences?"

"That will probably cost more," Yvette said.

She was standing in the kitchen, a glass of wine in one hand and a coffee in the other. Her dark hair had been tied back, and suddenly Jacob had an image of her curled up on his couch in front of a fire place, having a friendly debate about the best way to expand their business. To his surprise, the thought very much pleased him. He knew that if he was a sane person, he should get up right then and excuse himself for the evening, but instead he grabbed the wine bottle.

"More?" he asked both Faith and Yvette.

"Yes, please," Faith shoved her glass in front of him.

Yvette eyed hers then shook her head with a frown. "I've already gone past my one glass limit, and I have to drive home."

"Oh, come on Vette," Faith said, giggling. "I'm sure Jacob can give you a lift if you get a little tipsy. He already knows where you live."

"You did not just say that," Yvette said, staring her sister down.

Faith slapped her hand over her mouth. "Oops, guess I'm the one who's had one too many."

Jacob put the wine bottle back on the counter and said, "Maybe we've all had enough for the evening."

"I think you might be right." Yvette swiped the glasses off the counter and took them to the sink.

"I'm sorry," Faith said, her smile too wide to indicate any sort of sincerity. "It just slipped out."

"It's fine." Jacob said. "I think that's my cue to head out."

"Oh, no. But it's so early," Faith said.

"No, it isn't," Yvette said as she glanced at the wall clock. "It's already past nine, and dad needs his rest."

Past nine? Seriously? Jacob thought. He should've realized it was getting late. Noel and Drew had packed the girls up and had taken off over an hour ago, and Lin had retreated to his couch with Clair where the pair were watching an old John Wayne movie. He stood and glanced at Yvette. "I'll see you tomorrow?"

She crossed through the kitchen and rounded the counter as she said, "I'll walk you out."

"G'night, Jacob," Faith said, waving her fingers at him. "Thanks for the advice. I really appreciate it."

"Sure, Faith. It was my pleasure," he said.

"Don't keep encouraging her," Yvette whispered as she slipped her arm through his and tugged him toward the door.

"Why? You don't think the spa is a good idea?" he asked her.

"It's not that. Not at all. It's just that you'll never get rid of her now, and the next thing you know, she'll be asking advice on which scents to buy."

"I heard that," Faith called out good naturedly. "And you're wrong. I already have a handle on fragrances."

"That's something at least," Yvette called over her shoulder, her eyes glinting with mischief.

Jacob watched the sisterly exchange with amusement and a little bit of envy. He hadn't had siblings while growing up. He had two step-brothers now, but they only saw each other during rare family events and had never had the opportunity to form the bond the Townsend family obviously had with each other. It made his chest ache just a little with what he'd so clearly missed out on.

"Goodnight, Jacob. I'm glad you could come tonight," Lin said as he pushed himself up off the couch. The older man held his hand out. "It was a pleasure getting to know you better."

"You too, sir," Jacob said, clasping the other man's hand with both of his. "You have a lovely home and family." He tipped his head to Clair. "Sorry if I've overstayed my welcome."

"Of course not, son," Lin said. "I'm not that old. Besides, I'm still waiting for my son-in-law to drop off some paperwork I've been waiting for in regard to the orchard."

Yvette stiffened. Her tone turned icy as she said, "*Son-in-law?* Please tell me you aren't talking about Isaac."

Lin winced. "Sorry, Yvette. Ex son-in-law. Isaac still does the bookkeeping for the farm. I needed some forms for a meeting tomorrow. He's supposed to drop them by after his dinner."

"You need a new bookkeeper, Dad," Faith said. All of her earlier amusement had vanished, and she was now giving her father a disapproving look. "He can't keep coming around here. It's not fair to Yvette."

Lin turned to Yvette, worry in his expression. "Is that what you want me to do, Rusty? I know we talked about this and—"

"It's fine," Yvette said, cutting him off. "Of course I don't want you to fire Isaac because our relationship didn't work out. Just... maybe give me a heads up when I might be running into him."

"Are you sure?" Lin asked her.

"Of course I am," she said, but her clenched fists and her tight jaw made it clear she wasn't nearly as Zen with the situation as she was trying to portray. "I just need some time to get used to it, and it would help if you stopped saying son-in-law."

"It won't happen again," Lin said with a resolute nod.

"Okay then. Good night," she said. "Dad, make sure you don't work too hard."

Lin muttered some sort of half-hearted agreement as Yvette tugged Jacob out the front door. Her movements were stiff, and she was muttering something about someone being a jackass under her breath.

"Are you referring to your ex or just men in general?" Jacob asked, trying to lighten the mood a little as the door behind them clicked closed.

She let out a startled huff of laughter. "You know, I'm honestly not sure. In what world is it fair that he got half the value of my bookstore and he gets to keep my family, too? And what did I get? A house I used to love, but now can't stand to live in, and a new business partner who—" She glanced up at him and grimaced. "Sorry. This isn't a rant about you."

"Sounds like it might be a little bit about me, but it's okay. I completely understand."

She stopped in the middle of the porch and turned to face him. Her eyes searched his as she asked, "Do you really?"

He nodded, feeling the familiar anger he'd suppressed deep in his gut. It made him want to tear down everything and everyone who'd walked all over him, used him for their own gains. "I wasn't married, but I was engaged. And let's just say my fiancée walked away with everything she wanted, including my best man."

Yvette's mouth dropped open in shock as she stared up at him.

His mouth went dry as he heard his words ringing in his ears. Why had he just told her that? He hadn't told anyone about Sienna and Brian. Not even his lawyer who was working out the dissolution of the business they'd started as well as the division of the beach house Jacob had purchased for them. He just hadn't been able to say the words before.

"That's awful," Yvette said, lightly placing a hand on his arm. "I'm sorry. That's really messed up."

"Yeah, well, so is marrying the woman you claim is your best friend then running off with another man and thinking nothing has changed other than who you live with." A lock of her hair had fallen from the impromptu bun. He brushed it off her cheek and tucked it behind her ear. "I'm willing to bet Isaac is so self-involved he has no idea how much it hurts you to see him at all, let alone see him with his new partner, or when he's pretending he's still part of your family."

Silver moonlight poked through the coastal clouds and illuminated her pretty face. A small contemplative frown had claimed her lips as she stared up at him. "You know, I think you're right. I mean, he realizes he hurt me. He's apologized more times than I can count. But he wants—and to be honest everyone else wants—for me to just get over it. Everyone keeps telling me to move on and let him be happy in his life. And I want to. I really do. We really were best friends. I understand he didn't intentionally try to cause me pain, but the truth is it still hurts. I can't rush the healing no matter how much I want to."

"I know," he said, softly caressing her cheek.

The sound of a car door slamming startled both of them. Yvette jumped back then peered into the darkness. "Isaac, is that you?"

"It's me," he barked as he stepped out of the shadows. "I'm just here to see Lin."

"Exactly how long were you sitting there watching us?" Yvette asked, her hands on her hips and her eyes narrowed to slits. It had to have been since they before they exited the house, otherwise she would've heard his car as he drove up the lane.

"I wasn't watching you," he said. "I was gathering the paperwork that spilled into the floorboard of my car. But if I had been, I'd tell you that you're making a huge mistake rushing into whatever this is with your *business partner*. Really, Yvette? You can't honestly think that's a good idea."

Yvette gaped at him and shook her head in disbelief.

Jacob took a step forward, purposely invading Isaac's personal space. "I'm fairly positive that it's no longer any of your business what Yvette does. Maybe you should keep your opinions to yourself, huh, buddy?"

"Of course it's my business. I'm her husband," Isaac said, backing away and moving to the side to distance himself from the taller man.

"Ex-husband!" Yvette shouted. "Ex-husband, Isaac. We've both signed the paperwork. It's been mailed in. You don't get to act like I belong to you just because the divorce decree hasn't come in the mail yet. Stop acting like you have a say in anything or *anyone* I do."

"Anyone?" Isaac shot back, his eyes flashing with anger. "Come on, Yvette. Don't be crass. You know full well I'm only looking out for you."

What a condescending piece of work, Jacob thought. Was this guy serious? Jacob's muscles involuntarily flexed, and it was all he could do to hold himself back from decking the guy. If Jacob had been younger, he might have. But with age came at least a little bit of wisdom. Violence wasn't going to do anything but escalate the situation. Besides, Yvette was already handling things pretty well.

Yvette moved across the yard and stopped right in front of Isaac. Her body was trembling with what Jacob assumed was anger when she leaned in and said, "Do not ever tell me what to do again. I'm not yours to look out for, and I do not appreciate your condescending tone. You gave up any rights to have an opinion about what I do the day you served me with divorce papers."

"Yvette," Isaac said, reaching out to touch her shoulder.

She jerked away. "Don't touch me. I'm done here." Yvette turned to Jacob. "Ready?"

"Absolutely," he said, mildly surprised when she walked over to his truck. Without a word, he opened the passenger door for her and then couldn't help himself as he sent Isaac a self-satisfied smile as he made his way back to the driver's side.

"Sorry," she said, shaking her head as soon as he took his place behind the wheel. "I'm so angry right now, I don't think I should be driving."

"No problem." He cranked the engine and eased the truck down the long driveway that led to the main road.

Yvette pulled the visor down and let out an annoyed huff. "He's just standing there on the porch watching us leave."

"Of course he is." Jacob smiled at her. "He's jealous."

She rolled her eyes. "Yeah, I thought that too at first, but now I just think his ego is bruised. I mean, come on, he's clearly in love with another man."

"It's not just ego. I'm telling you, he's definitely jealous. It's obvious."

She turned in her seat, giving Jacob her full attention. "You really think so?"

"Yvette, he obviously loved you if he married you. That probably didn't change just because he realized he's gay. The man is definitely jealous. Whether he admits it or not, he hates seeing you with another man."

"Hmm." She tapped one red-painted finger nail against her lips. Then she smiled and said, "Good. Let him suffer a little."

He laughed. "That's the spirit."

CHAPTER 8

Considering her blow up with Isaac the night before, Yvette had slept surprisingly well. Jacob had managed to calm her down and had even been a complete gentleman when he'd dropped her off at home. He'd offered to pick her up and take her to work, but she'd declined, preferring to not put him out in any way.

Instead, she dressed warmly in jeans and a sweater and pulled on her fur-lined boots. Then she topped her outfit with a red wool jacket, gray gloves, and a matching scarf and freed her bike from the garage. The morning was overcast and cold with a slight drizzle, but nothing she couldn't handle. The cold air stung her cheeks as she rode through the streets of Keating Hollow, and even though it was gray and drizzly, she couldn't help but admire her quaint town.

Twinkle lights lit the lampposts, and most of the storefronts were still decorated with fake snow and holiday greetings. She knew by the end of the week, all of it would be gone, replaced by displays for the New Year Witch's festival.

Soon after, everything would be decorated with red and pink hearts and snippets of poems suitable for Valentine's Day. The realization made Yvette groan.

The residents of Keating Hollow loved Valentine's Day. There was no escaping it. It would be everywhere. Miss Maple would start serving heart shaped cupcakes complete with love spell chocolate hearts, the brewery would roll out Clay's signature Love Potion Brew, and the restaurants would start advertising their special Valentine's Day dinner menus and taking reservations within days. Usually they booked up within the hour and had waiting lists dozens of people deep. Meanwhile, Yvette would fill her front windows with romances, stock the store with plenty of roses, eat a vat of chocolate caramels, and count down the days until February fifteenth.

It was still early, and with the exception of Incantation Café, most of the businesses on Main Street weren't even open yet. Yvette wasn't expecting anyone to already be at the store, but when she parked her bike out front she noticed two things: Jacob's truck was already there, and the front window was animated.

She let out a small gasp as she turned her attention to the window. The books she'd placed there the day before were all suspended and slowing rocking back and forth as if they were caught in a slight breeze. Below, on the bay windowsill where she'd created a small village and added cute felted witches, werewolves, and vampires, the creatures were paired up and dancing in the street.

"It just needs the twinkle lights and a harvest moon, and the window will be complete," Jacob said from behind her.

She jumped, startled by his voice. "How long have you been there?"

"Just a minute." He held up a bag that had *Incantation Café* scrawled across the front. "I got us some scones to go with our coffee."

She eyed the bag. "There's no way you have coffee cups in there."

He grinned. "Nope, but I do have espresso grounds to go with the fancy new machine that showed up after you left yesterday. Brinn left a note with the parcel on the counter for us, and I found it this morning."

"That was fast," she said, both impressed and mildly annoyed once again that he'd ordered the machine without even asking her. But she took a deep breath and put that out of her mind. They'd already come to terms with the bookstore café. It was time to let it go. "Did you do this?" she asked as she waved at the window display.

"Yes," he said, watching her closely. He was obviously gauging her reaction as he added, "I saw it this morning and thought it could use something. What do you think?"

"It's perfect!" She grinned up at him. "Yesterday I was thinking I needed an air witch to give it that something special, but you'd left for the day and… well, there wasn't time to call my sister, and Brinn's talents aren't quite elegant enough for what I'd imagined. What was that you were saying about the moon and twinkle lights?" She peered back into the window.

"The display is great during the day, but if you give it some candlelight, then when it gets dark out, it's going to be really fantastic. You're a fire witch, right? Are you up for it?"

"Say no more." Yvette strode into the store. After rummaging through her window display supplies, she found a package of small white birthday candles and a round piece of wood she'd once used for the base of a miniature Yule tree. She returned to the window and handed them to Jacob. "Make the wood float in the left-hand corner above the town and place the candles so they're hovering in the windows of the buildings."

"Got it." Jacob tossed the supplies in the air. The candles lined up in front of him as if they were waiting for instructions while the piece of wood bobbed off to the side. He snapped his fingers and each candle went exactly where it was supposed to go, while the faux moon glided into place as if it had read Yvette's mind instead of Jacob's.

Yvette first focused on the moon. She envisioned embers glowing from the inside and just like that, the wood piece glowed orange. "Perfect."

"Is the fire trapped inside?" Jacob asked as he admired her handiwork.

"Yes, but it's a magical flame, so it's contained. No chance of the wood going up in flames." She turned her attention to the candles. Holding her hand up to her mouth in a loose fist, she blew a bit of air into the window. A tiny light flew from her lips and zoomed around to each of the candles, lighting the wicks as if a firefly had done all the work. She turned to Jacob. "What do you think?"

He chuckled. "You really do have a fire lit inside of you."

"That's what you get when you hang with a fire witch." She winked then picked up the bag from Incantation Café that he'd left on a nearby shelf. "Tell me there's a bear claw in here."

"Does magic make you hungry?"

"Always," she said, peeking into the bag. "Oh, my goodness!" She pulled out a cookie that was shaped just like the store front of the bookstore. It had the words *Hollow Books* piped across the top and a red door that was just like the shop's entryway. "I can't believe they already started working on stuff for us. Did Hanna do this?"

"Yep. Go ahead, try it," he said as he moved to the far counter where he'd already set up the espresso machine.

Yvette took a small bite, and as soon as the gingerbread hit her mouth, the spices exploded over her tongue, causing her to let out a moan of pleasure.

"That was my reaction," Jacob said as he worked the espresso machine like an expert.

"I can't believe how good these are," Yvette said and took another, larger bite. She was so engrossed in the cookie, she barely even noticed when Jacob set a latte in front of her. She gave him a nod and washed the rest of the cookie down with a healthy gulp of the latte. She had to admit, it was good. Excellent in fact. "You were right," she conceded. "A bookstore café is exactly what we needed. Between these cookies and whatever else they come up with and fresh coffee, we're going to be a huge hit with the book browsing crowd."

He raised his own latte in acknowledgement then said, "You're the one who came up with custom pastries. You deserve all the credit for that. Completely inspired, my new friend."

But Yvette shook her head. "This is all Hanna. All I did was request something fun for the store." She set her latte on the counter and bit down on her lower lip. "There is something I need to tell you."

He guided her to a nearby overstuffed couch and waved for her to take a seat. When she was settled, he sat down next to her. He had a faint, pleasant, woodsy scent that made her wonder if he'd gotten a place out in the redwoods. "Shoot. I'm all ears."

"Well, I made a blunder. A pretty big one. And I would've told you sooner, but I discovered it yesterday after you'd left, and dinner didn't seem like the best time to bring it up."

"Okay," he said as he furrowed his brow, concentrating on her. "How big of a blunder are we talking here?"

"It depends on your definition of big," she said.

"So it does. Why don't you just tell me whatever it is, and we'll go from there." He had his arms crossed over his chest and was all business now as he watched her, stone-faced.

She had the urge to scoot back or clear her throat, but she did neither. Instead she swallowed her anxiety and blurted, "I massively over-ordered books that aren't returnable... and after I paid the invoices yesterday, our current cash on hand is dangerously low."

He blinked. Then his cheeks started to turn red with what she had to assume was irritation. "Non-returnable?"

She nodded. "Small and micro presses don't do print runs, only print-on-demand. I... um... dang it! Isaac used to do all the ordering, and I was unfamiliar with the ordering software and just messed up. It won't happen again. Trust me. I'm a fast learner."

"I'm familiar with small and micro publishers," he said.

"Okay. Well anyway, I did try to return some, but as expected, that was a nonstarter. So I came up with a plan on how to move these books." She leaned in, projecting every ounce of confidence she could find. "Want to hear it?"

"I can't wait," he said, shaking his head in what she assumed was disbelief.

"First things first. The window is done. Thank you for your help. I think it will get a lot of attention."

"That's the hope," he said and leaned back in his chair as he scrutinized Yvette. "But you know that a display's main purpose is to get customers in the store. It doesn't always translate to more sales of whatever we're advertising."

"Right. I'm well aware of that," Yvette said. "That's why the window was just the first step." She pulled out a flyer that was an advertisement for Keating Hollow's New Year Witch's Festival. "This is happening this weekend, and the town is going to fill up with a bunch of tourists. Noel says her inn is completely booked, and so is the Book and Stone, the large Victorian that was turned into a bed and breakfast a few years ago. And I happen to know that Miranda Moon lives somewhere in Northern California. I was thinking maybe we could invite her to do a signing and advertise it around town. Maybe get Hanna to make some cookies that resemble the emblem on her books?"

"It's already Tuesday," Jacob said.

She blinked at him. "Is that your only response? It's already Tuesday?"

He glanced at his watch and nodded. "That gives us maybe four days to track down the author, get paperwork signed, find a room for her—"

"She can stay at my house," Yvette said. "I have the space. And it's free."

"That's something at least." He pulled out his phone, made a quick phone call to someone named Fran, and then ended up with Miranda Moon's personal phone number.

"How did you do that?" She tilted her head to the side, studying him. "Have you met Miranda?"

He nodded. "Sure. At a conference once or twice before. And she was friends with my ex. I got her number from our former wedding planner. Miranda was supposed to be a bridesmaid."

Yvette groaned. "You can't be serious."

He let out a humorless laugh. "Oh, I'm quite serious. Let me give her a call and see what I can do."

Five minutes later, Jacob ended the call with a triumphant grin. "Miranda will be here Friday afternoon. She'll stay for the festival through the weekend to meet fans and sign however many books come across her path."

"How did you do that?" Yvette asked with a smirk. "She couldn't see you, so it couldn't be your charming smile or somewhat-decent looks."

"Somewhat-decent looks?" He let out a loud laugh. "You're not fooling anyone, Townsend. I still remember Saturday night."

She flushed. "Never mind. I have work to do. I'm going to make postcards and flyers for all the local business, then I need to get the word out online." She started to move back toward her office, but after a few steps she paused and glanced back. "I'm sorry about the blunder. It won't happen again. I promise."

He tilted his head to the side and studied her. "Yvette, are you under the impression I'm upset?"

"Yeah, I guess. Why wouldn't you be? I made a giant error, and now we're scrambling to figure out how to sell these extra books instead of settling in and working on new ideas for the store."

"This *is* a new idea," he said. "Book signings, especially with local writers, is a huge boost for us and for them. I'd like to plan at least one a month for the foreseeable future. And for the record, I'm not mad. Not even a little bit. Concerned about cash flow? Yes. But we'll work it out. I'm not perfect, and I don't expect you to be either. Everyone makes mistakes. Owning up to them is the most important part. And it's fair to say you did more than that, so thank you." He held out his hand, waiting for her to take it, but instead, she threw her arms around him and gave him a tight hug.

"Whoa," he said, caught off guard, but he quickly wrapped his arms around her, embracing her.

"Thanks," she said into his shoulder. "If this is how you handle things, then I think we're going to make a great pair."

"Does this mean our partnership is going to involve hugging on a semi-regular basis? Because I could really be on board with that," he teased.

"Sure." She giggled. "Just as long as you keep me supplied in cookies and lattes, it'd be my pleasure."

"No, Yvette, the pleasure would certainly be all mine," he said into her ear, sending a shiver all the way to her toes.

CHAPTER 9

Jacob spent the morning stocking the shelves with the inventory that was crowding his soon-to-be new office. His first order of business was to create a couple of display tables for the mountain of Miranda Moon books that Yvette had ordered.

He had to admit, he had been slightly alarmed when she'd first told him about her mistake. Bookstores were notorious for running on slim margins, and Hollow Books was no exception. He believed there were steps they could take to significantly grow the business, but if they were careless, they wouldn't be in business long enough to even try.

But the fact that she'd told him immediately and stepped up with a plan to move the excess inventory had reaffirmed why he'd gone into business with her in the first place. When he'd spoken with her over the phone a few weeks ago, he'd found her smart and passionate and completely invested—the three things he believed business owners needed to be in order to succeed. But those weren't the only reasons he'd taken a chance on Hollow Books. His aunt had been a major force, and so had his need to get the heck out of southern California. There'd been a lot of reasons to say yes, and only one to say no. The yeses had won.

If his life with Sienna hadn't blown up, he couldn't have seen himself investing in a place like Hollow Books. It wasn't ever going to be more than a small-town bookstore, and that more than anything made the place a bad fit… or it had until the crap had hit the fan. Then he'd suddenly found himself longing for something simple. Something that meant *more*… something other than profits.

He just wondered how long he'd be content in the small town, running a single store, and not out making his mark on the business world. Time would certainly tell, but for now, he was thoroughly enjoying hanging out with his fiery business partner.

"Yvette," he called. "Stop eating the cookies. We have books to stack."

She was holding a cookie in one hand and a napkin in the other. "I have to eat them, otherwise there won't be any left. *Someone* keeps swiping them on his way back to the storage room."

He laughed. She was right. He couldn't help himself; they were *that* good. "Just put it down. I could use another hand. I promise I won't eat your share."

She gave him a skeptical look but placed the cookie on her napkin and turned to wash her hands in the small wall sink where the new café would be. Jacob stared at the almost-intact cookie and seriously considered swiping it before she turned back around, but his hands were full of books and he really did need her help.

"Okay," she said. "What do you need?"

"See those books there?" He nodded to a pile of books in

front of him. "I need you to stack them right in the middle of this table."

"Okay. Now what?" she asked after she was done.

He dropped the large stack of books he'd been holding in the newly cleared space and explained how he wanted the table arranged for maximum exposure.

"I'm all over it." She went to work, placing the books in a variety of positions so that visitors would see the covers from many different angles. When she was done with her section, she retreated to the door and studied the table with a critical eye. "It's too much signage. We should take one of the banners down… the one on the left. And all the books on the right need to be shifted two or three inches. There, that's it," she said as Jacob did what she asked. "Perfect."

He took a moment to study the table from her view and once he did, he was again very impressed with her eye for detail. He almost felt as if they were a match made in heaven. It also made him wonder why she'd been so upset after ordering too many books. As far as he could tell, she was everything he'd thought she was: smart, passionate, and committed. She didn't need to worry about what he was thinking. She was damned good at her job.

But then just after one o'clock in the afternoon, Jacob discovered the answer as to why Yvette had let his reaction bother her so much. He'd moved on to stocking the shelves with their latest inventory when, wouldn't you know it, Isaac Santini walked in and immediately spotted the elaborate display of Miranda Moon books.

"What is this?" he called as he stared in Yvette's direction.

"A display of books," she said calmly. "You should check them out. Moon's books are fun, romantic, and full of heart."

"Yvette, you know the store can't carry that much inventory. It's irresponsible. What are you trying to do? Put yourself out of business?" He picked one up and eyed the spine. Groaning, he added, "You can't even return these for credit."

She crossed her arms over her chest and glared at him. "Was there something you needed besides telling me what a terrible businessperson I am?"

"That's not—" he started.

Yvette grabbed the book out of his hand and placed it back on the table. "You should leave. We have nothing to say to each other."

Jacob moved to stand right behind Yvette, ready to back her up in case she decided her ex needed to be escorted off the property.

"I'm here to get a gift," he said with a heavy sigh. "Jeez, Yvette. Don't tank the store just because you're angry with me."

"We don't need your business," she said and pointed to the door.

"Clearly you do," he said, eyeing the large display.

Yvette opened her mouth to dispute him, but Jacob spoke before she could get any words out.

"Actually, Isaac," Jacob said, "we don't. And the large inventory is part of the new business plan that we're excited to roll out. Sorry we didn't run it by you first, but since you are no longer an owner, we figured it wasn't necessary. But thanks for your concern." He placed his hands on Yvette's shoulders, mostly out of reflex as a protective maneuver. But when Isaac's eyes flashed with irritation, Jacob smiled, satisfied that he'd pissed the other guy off. "Now, what was it you needed? I'm sure Brinn would be happy to help you find whatever it is."

Isaac ignored Jacob's question and focused on Yvette. "I don't know what's going on between you two, but I do know that when it doesn't work out, you're going to regret it. And I won't be coming around to pick up the pieces."

Jacob could feel Yvette's skin burning straight through her

thick sweater. He was certain Isaac's condescension had lit her inner fire. But instead of lashing out at her ex, she turned to Jacob and put her hand on his chest.

"Awe, isn't it sweet? Now he's worried about me. What do you say, Jacob? Should I be worried about you breaking my heart?"

Considering they'd both decided they should keep their relationship strictly professional, there was little chance of that. He shook his head. "No. Not at all."

"See?" she said to Isaac. "We're all good here." Then without warning, she turned back to Jacob, lifted up on her tiptoes, and pressed her lips to his.

He stood there frozen for just a second, trying to get his brain to engage. He was not supposed to be kissing her again. But then he quickly realized this was just a show to further annoy her ex, and he was all in. He wrapped both arms around her waist, parted his lips, and deepened the kiss with an obvious spark of passion. She tasted of sweet gingerbread as her tongue met his, and her fire flickered through him like a gentle flame, warming him from the inside out.

Isaac and the bookstore seemed to fade into the background as all of his focus turned to the soft, pliant woman wrapped around him. The kiss turned tender, and he felt as if he could be content to stay in that moment for forever. He would have, too, if it hadn't been for her ex clearing his throat.

Yvette pulled back but kept her hands fisted in his shirt as she gazed up at him. Her expression was soft and slightly awed. There was no denying that the kiss had all but knocked him right off his axis.

"I think you've both made your point," Isaac said. "Yvette, I hope you know what you're doing." He spun on his heel and stormed out of the store.

"I think we just lost a customer," Yvette said, her eyes twinkling with mischief.

"It was worth it," he said as he stared down at her rosy lips.

The clock ticked loudly in the silent room, and it was as if the sound had broken whatever spell had come over them. They both stepped back at the same time.

Yvette gently covered her lips with her fingertips as she averted her gaze. "Books on fire," she muttered. "I shouldn't have done that."

"Which part?" he asked, already regretting letting her go. "Deliberately irritating your ex or kissing your business partner?"

She winced as she made eye contact again. "The kissing part. We're… that's not what we should be doing. I'm sorry. It won't happen again."

Disappointment crashed through him, and he wanted to say *he* wasn't sorry. Not one little bit. And that given the chance, he'd do it all over again. But he didn't. They'd agreed that a romantic relationship wasn't a good idea. She'd already almost lost her store once because her marriage broke up. And he'd lost Enchanted Bliss the same way. If they got together, once the relationship blew up, they'd be stuck in the same mess. And it would blow up. Relationships always did.

"No apology necessary," he said with a cocky smile, trying to act as if she hadn't just rocked his world. "I was happy to help."

"I bet you were," she said with a teasing eye roll. "Just don't get used to it. Believe it or not, I'm not in the habit of just kissing random guys. Usually I wait until we've at least had a first date."

"We've had a first date… sort of," he said with a shrug.

She blinked at him. Then she shook her head as she

chuckled. "I hate to tell you this, Jacob, but hooking up with a stranger after a wedding is definitely not a date."

"It's not?" He clutched his chest over his heart and pretended to be offended. "But that's the way I meet all my girlfriends."

"No wonder you're single," she said with a laugh.

"That's cold, Townsend." He shook his head. "What about dinner at your dad's house? That was almost a blind date."

She snorted and patted his chest. "Oh, you poor misguided thing. One day when you meet a nice girl you'd like to keep around, remind me to give you some dating instructions. Until then, let's just get back to work, okay?"

"Anything you say, boss," he said as he reached over and stole the cookie she'd left on the table.

CHAPTER 10

The sun had already set when Yvette walked back into the bookstore just after five, and she was surprised to see the place packed with customers. She'd taken the afternoon to run out to Eureka to pick up the flyers and postcards she'd ordered for the signing Miranda Moon had graciously offered to attend that weekend. When she'd left, there'd only been one person in the store—Shannon Ansell. The woman worked half a block down at A Spoonful of Magic for Miss Maple, Jacob's aunt. And Yvette had known right away the curvy redhead hadn't been there for the books. She'd come in to check out Keating Hollow's newest eligible bachelor.

Shannon had spent a good twenty minutes fawning all over Jacob, praising him for the book he'd written and clutching his arm while she insisted he show her around, as if she couldn't possibly find her way to the mystery section. After watching Shannon pet his chest for the third time, Yvette had escaped. It was better than clawing the other woman's eyes out over a man she'd told herself was completely off-limits.

Yvette walked up to the counter where Brinn was ringing up a transaction. She smiled at the older woman across the counter. "Hello, Ms. Betty, what brings you into the store today? Looking for more botany books?"

"Oh no. I have plenty of those, and my winter garden is doing outstandingly well. The lettuce is taking over." She leaned in and lowered her voice. "That sassy girl that works at Miss Maple's came by the bingo hall and mentioned a yummy new neighbor, so that got all of us in to see what we'd been missing." She glanced over at Jacob, who was surrounded by a half-dozen senior citizens. After fanning herself she added, "He's something else, isn't he?"

"He's certainly something," Brinn said, doing her best to remain diplomatic about her boss.

Yvette chuckled and eyed the bag of books Brinn had passed to the woman. "Did you get him to help you pick something out?"

"Absolutely. He told me I just had to read the newest series by Miranda Moon, and then of course I grabbed a couple of Nora's newest releases as well. Can't go wrong with a good romance, especially when someone like that handsome man is helping you pick them out."

"Excellent. Thanks for stopping by. I hope it was well worth the effort," Yvette said.

"Oh, sweetie, you have no idea." She flashed a wicked little smile before shuffling back over to Jacob and her mob of friends fawning all over him.

Yvette turned to Brinn, her eyes wide with disbelief. "Can you believe this?"

Brinn laughed. "Yes. Have you not spent *any* time down at the bingo hall? The ladies spend a lot of time talking about the hotties in town."

"No, I can't say that I have. If I'd known they were all going to go gaga over Jacob, I'd have turned this meet-and-greet into a catered party."

"Now that's an idea," Brinn said as she smiled at another one of the bingo hall ladies.

The woman's arms were overflowing with books and as Yvette helped her stack them on the counter, she wasn't surprised to see all four of Miranda Moon's among the pile. Jacob was really working at moving that inventory.

It was another half-hour before Yvette took pity on Jacob and decided to rescue him from his newest fans. And she was just in time too. As she was making her way over to the group, she spied Ms. Betty slipping her arm around Jacob's waist. He smiled at her patiently, but then she leaned in, giving him a side hug, and covertly slipped her hand down to his butt and squeezed.

He let out a yelp and jumped back, nearly knocking over the freshly-dyed redhead who was standing on his left-hand side.

"Betty, for goodness sake, what are you trying to do, get the young man all worked up?" the redhead said. "You know you can't just go grabbing them in public. It makes them too excited. Don't you remember what happened to Billy Blue when you did that to him a couple of years ago? His pecker stood straight up, and he was forever known as Billy Blue Balls until he moved to Eureka." She patted Jacob's arm and gave him a sympathetic smile. "You wouldn't want Jacob here ending up with a name like Jack in the Pants just because you couldn't keep your magical hands to yourself, now would you?"

Jacob let out an audible groan.

"See, now he's uncomfortable," the redhead said, eyeing his groin area. "Though I'm not seeing much evidence of a wood—"

"Okay, ladies," Yvette said, slipping in between Jacob and Ms. Betty. "I hate to break up the party, but it's already after closing hours, and Jacob and I still have some work to do before we head out for the evening. Are there any last-minute items anyone needs before we lock up?"

"Oh, gosh. Time sure does fly when you're flirting with your new favorite bookseller," Ms. Betty said. "Girls, we better get going, otherwise George over at the bingo hall is going to put out an APB on us."

The women milled about, calling their goodbyes to Jacob as they slowly made their way out of the store. When the last one finally exited, Yvette waved goodbye, thanked them for coming in, and then shut and locked the door. After flipping the sign to closed, she turned and eyed Jacob, who was sitting in one of the overstuffed chairs with his forearm covering his eyes.

She glanced over at Brinn where she was closing out the register, and they both started to laugh.

"I can hear you," he said.

His statement only made them laugh harder.

"You two are despicable," he said, but Yvette could hear the humor in his tone.

She crossed the room and took a seat next to him. "I'm sorry. We shouldn't have laughed."

He put his arm down and looked at her. "Why not? It was funny as hell."

"You were sexually assaulted by a seventy-something-year-old woman, and we didn't do anything."

"Sure, you did. You got them out of here." He pushed himself out of the chair and got to his feet. "Don't worry about it. I can handle it." He started to move back toward the offices, but she gently grabbed his arm, stopping him.

"Let me at least make it up to you. Dinner? We can head

over to Woodlines for some seafood, maybe share a bottle of wine?"

He lowered his gaze to where her hand was resting on his arm. Then he looked up and said, "Is this one of those dates we said we wouldn't go on?"

She quickly dropped her hand and shook her head. "Consider it a business dinner. We can talk about ways to get more locals in that don't involve pimping you out to the senior citizen crowd."

He chuckled. "That's a compelling argument. All right, I'm in."

"Excellent. Let me just grab my things, and we can go."

They both retreated to their offices and met back at the front door, outerwear in hand. Yvette glanced over at Brinn. "Are you good? Do you need anything before we go?"

She waved them off. "I'm just about set. Enjoy your dinner. I'll lock up as usual."

"Thanks," Yvette said. "G'night."

"Night, Brinn. Thanks for everything today," Jacob added.

"No problem. I'll see you tomorrow."

Once they were out on the street, Jacob glanced at the bike Yvette had left in the rack to the left of the entrance. "You're not riding that home tonight."

"Why not?" she asked. "My place isn't that far."

"It's too foggy. Unlock it and I'll put it in the back of my truck. I'll drop you off after dinner."

She glanced around at the thickening fog and knew it would likely only get worse. "Yeah, okay."

After they got the bike secured in the truck, Jacob opened the passenger door for her.

She couldn't help the warm, fuzzy feeling that blossomed in her chest. It had been a long time since she'd been out with anyone so gentlemanly. "Thank you," she said as she climbed in.

He hurried around to the other side and a few moments later, they were headed down toward the other end of Main Street. "So, this non-date… do we have ground rules?" he asked as he made sure to point one of the heater vents in her direction.

"Just that I'm paying. It's only fair since you had to endure the bingo ladies."

"That's the only ground rule?" he asked, raising one curious eyebrow.

"Well, besides the obvious. No groping, leering, or inappropriate sexual innuendo," she said.

"How about flirting?" he asked as he pulled the truck into a space right in front of Woodlines.

"A little flirting is fine," she said with a laugh. There was no reason to turn this into a sterile business meeting. She did after all, really enjoy their banter.

"How do you feel about sharing dessert? Can our forks cross?"

She snorted her amusement. "Now you're just being silly. Of course, your fork has to stay on your side of the plate, but I will share my pie with you."

"Pie. Interesting," he said with a small smirk.

"Hey!" She pointed a finger at him. "I said no inappropriate sexual innuendo."

"You started it." He jumped out of the truck and jogged around to her side, opening the door before she even got her seatbelt unbuckled.

She took the hand he held out for her and let him help her down out of the truck. When her feet were planted firmly on the ground, his fingers tightened around hers as he closed the door and then led her toward the restaurant. Yvette glanced down at their entwined fingers and knew she should pull her hand away, but she couldn't bring herself to do it. There was comfort in his touch, a comfort that she hadn't known she'd missed until that moment.

It didn't take long for them to be seated. Weeknights in early January in Keating Hollow were almost always low key, and that night was no exception. They sat across from each other, drinking wine and eating crab cakes while laughing about the bingo babes who'd fawned all over him for almost an hour.

"Your ego must've gotten quite a boost," Yvette said and took a sip of wine.

"Definitely. That was right about when you turned into a green-eyed monster and forced all of your competition out into the cold."

Yvette threw her head back and laughed. She couldn't remember the last time she'd been so relaxed and had just plain enjoyed herself when she'd been out with a man. Even though she and Isaac had only begun having problems a few months earlier, they hadn't had a fun night out in a very long time. A night that was full of friendship, laughter, and pure joy.

Had they ever had this much fun together? She knew they must've at some point, but she sure couldn't remember any in recent history.

"You know, it's really fun hanging out with you," Jacob said, taking a forkful of her blueberry pie.

"You're not so bad yourself." Yvette wrapped her hands around her latte. "Do you think we should talk about the store? About how to get more locals in?"

"Sure." He picked up his coffee mug and sat back in his chair. "What do you think about having Bingo Club Thursdays? We could get Hanna to make bingo card cupcakes."

Yvette grinned. "Are you part of the jackpot? 'Cause you

know the main reason they'd come back is to see you jump when Ms. Betty gets inappropriate again."

Jacob grimaced, and an involuntary shudder ran through him. "No, definitely not. But I'll stick around and charm them as long as *you* protect me from any roving hands."

"Deal." She raised her mug to his in a toast.

"Now, who are you going to entertain?" he asked.

She shrugged. "No one wants to ogle me. But if I had Book Club Tuesdays paired with wine tastings, I bet we could draw a crowd of overworked, sleep-deprived adults for a couple hours. Plus, there's always Saturday afternoon story time. That gets the parents bringing their kids in."

"Sounds perfect. We'll put those three things on the schedule along with at least one book signing a month, and I'd imagine we're looking at twenty to thirty percent growth in the next six months."

"You're very optimistic," she said, not bothering to hide her skepticism. She had no doubt that regular meetings in the store and signings would help, she just didn't think they'd have near the impact he expected.

"You think so?" he asked as if he was reconsidering. Then he said, "Nah. We'll have the café up and running too."

"We're probably going to need part time help, especially since my assistant Dannika's maternity leave started this week," she said, already calculating what that would do to the payroll budget.

"Let's see how we do without that expense for now. I'll take care of the café if you'll pick up the slack on the retail side. And if we really need to, we can ask Brinn if she'll put in a few extra hours until Dannika comes back to work."

"Deal!" She offered him her hand for them to shake on it.

Jacob wrapped his fingers around hers, but instead of the

traditional handshake, he held on lightly and stroked the back of her hand with his thumb.

Tingles sent gooseflesh up her arm, and she closed her eyes as she reveled in his gentle touch. When she finally opened them, she found him studying her, his lips curved into a hint of a smile.

"What?" she asked.

"I was just thinking that I wish I'd met you before we went into business together, because I'm not quite sure I'm going to be able to walk away tonight when I take you home."

Heat washed over her, and she was certain that her entire body had flushed crimson. She opened her mouth, shut it, and then just shook her head.

"You know what, Yvette?" he asked, his voice suddenly raspy. "Your reaction tells me that you don't want me to leave you alone tonight."

She cleared her throat and shook her head. "You aren't supposed to be flirting with me, Jacob."

He let out a low chuckle, his eyes never leaving hers. "I'm not flirting, Yvette. I'm trying to seduce you."

Oh, hell, she thought as her body came alive and every inch of her seemed to ache for his touch again. Reluctantly, she pulled her hand from his and said, "You're coloring outside the lines, Jacob. Remember the ground rules?"

He propped his elbows on the table and leaned in closer. "I can already tell that rules are going to be broken. It's not a matter of if… it's just a matter of when."

Yvette got to her feet and stared down at him. "I'm not exactly a rule breaker."

He laughed. "I highly doubt that."

"You'll see." She strode away from the table just to get a little distance. Jacob had a way of sucking her into his orbit, and she could already tell that if she wasn't careful, she'd forget all about her rules and end up right in the middle of something messy.

"Is everything okay, Yvette?" Wyatt, their waiter, asked as she nearly bumped right into him.

"Yep." She smiled. "Dinner was wonderful. I just needed some air. But since I have you here, let me go ahead and take care of the check."

"It's already taken care of," he said.

"What?" She glanced over her shoulder at Jacob, who was watching her from his place at the table. He flashed her a triumphant smile, and she gritted her teeth as she shook her head at him. Then she turned back to Wyatt. "Never mind. It was great. Thank you."

"You're very welcome. You two lovebirds come back real soon, okay?" He hurried off to take care of another table of customers before she could correct him. Of course, he'd made the assumption they were together. They'd been holding hands and making googly eyes at each other all night.

Damn. There was no question about it—she was doomed.

Jacob appeared beside her and whispered, "Ready for me to take you home?"

"Yes," she breathed, knowing she sounded like she couldn't wait for him to rip her clothes off. She sucked in air and forced herself to reiterate, "But don't get any ideas. The evening ends at my front door."

"Whatever you say, Yvette." He clasped his hand around hers and led her back outside to his truck. The air had turned downright cold, and she shivered as the foggy mist seemed to permeate right through her clothes. "You're freezing." Jacob hurried her into the truck and ran around to his side. In just moments, he had the heat blasting and was headed back the other way toward her house.

"Dinner was excellent," she said. "Thank you."

"You're welcome." He flashed her a smile. "The food was great, and the wine was better, but my favorite part was making you laugh. You light up from the inside out, and I don't mind telling you, it's captivating."

Had he really called her captivating? What an incredible compliment. Her first instinct was to brush him off, tell him to stop flattering her, but she stopped herself. There wasn't anything but sincerity in his expression, and as she gazed at him, butterflies fluttered in her stomach. She pressed a hand to her abdomen and said, "Thank you. I think that might be the best compliment I've ever received."

"I'm just stating the truth."

A comfortable silence fell between them for the rest of the ride. Once Jacob pulled his truck to a stop in her driveway, he jumped out, retrieved her bike, and helped her store it in the garage. Then he walked her to her door.

"I hate to say it, but I'm not inviting you in tonight," Yvette said.

His lips twitched into a small smile. "Tonight? That implies, if I give it a little time, I've still got a shot."

She laughed. "You're relentless."

"Not usually, but some people are worth the effort."

Yvette's insides turned to complete mush, and she wondered how she was going to continue to resist him when he was so adorable.

"Don't worry, Yvette," he said as he wrapped one arm around her waist and pulled her in close. "I hear you loud and clear."

"It sure doesn't feel like it," she said, breathless and more than a little dazzled.

"Trust me, I do." He slowly leaned down, bringing his lips just inches from hers. "Do you mind if I kiss you goodnight?"

Her gaze locked on his full lips, and the last of her resolve vanished. Rather than answering, she closed the distance and kissed him instead.

His arm tightened around her, pulling her in closer, and he parted his lips, welcoming her. The kiss was slow and thorough and made her tingle from head to toe. And when he finally let her go, she was breathing heavily and more than ready to invite him in despite her earlier objections.

"Goodnight, Yvette," he whispered in her ear. "I'll see you in the morning."

She was speechless as she watched him retreat to his truck, climb in, and drive away. Standing on her front porch with the cold air making her shiver, she stared at the taillights and knew without a doubt that Jacob Burton was, one way or another, going to break her heart.

CHAPTER 11

"I think we're ready," Brinn said, eyeing the signing area Yvette had set up for Miranda Moon. "We just need the author and a line of readers, and we'll be all set."

Yvette leaned against the checkout counter and took a sip of the latte Jacob had made for her while she tried to ignore her anxiety over the upcoming weekend. "You think anyone will show up?"

Brinn gave Yvette her signature you've-got-to-be-kidding-me eye roll. "You've passed out postcards to every business within a sixty-mile radius, sent out two newsletters to the store's contact list, blasted social media, and managed to get the biggest radio station over in Eureka to hype the event multiple times. If that media blitz and the festival itself don't bring them in, nothing will."

"Oh, my!" Ms. Betty said as she emerged from the romance aisle, her arms laden with a stack of Kristen Painter paranormal romances. "It looks wonderful. I love how you've set up book displays by similar authors. I came in today because I loved those Miranda Moon books Jacob recommended. I couldn't wait to pick up more like them."

"That's what we like to hear," Yvette said with a smile, relieving the woman of her haul.

Brinn slipped behind the counter and started to ring up Ms. Betty's purchases while Yvette packed them in a canvas bag with the *Hollow Books* logo.

"Don't you worry about the turn-out tomorrow," Ms. Betty said. She placed a wrinkled hand on Yvette's arm, leaned in, and whispered, "I've been spreading the word about your handsome partner around town, and the ladies are dying to check him out. Our entire Eureka book club plans to be here. They couldn't resist after I told them how firm his buns are."

"Now Ms. Betty, you know you can't grope him again, right?" Yvette said, trying to nip the inappropriate behavior in the bud.

"Oh, I can if I get consent," she said, waving a hand as if she just knew that Jacob would welcome her advances. "My friend who teaches yoga out at the college filled me in on the new rules. She says it's all about communication now." She shook her head and let out a small chuckle. "She says I'm 'woke' now. I don't know what that means, but she seemed to think it's a good thing."

"It is a good thing," Yvette confirmed with a laugh. Then she sobered as she remembered Ms. Betty had invited all her friends to the event just to see Jacob. Yvette placed a hand on Ms. Betty's shoulder. "Listen, you might want to give your friends a heads-up that Jacob isn't going to be here. He's leaving in the morning for a weekend business meeting."

"Oh, no." Ms. Betty clasped her hand over her mouth. "This isn't good. Not good at all. I'll still show up of course, but there are a lot of women coming tomorrow just for a selfie with Mr. Handsome." She quickly paid for her books then grabbed the bag and said, "Thanks. I have to get going. Looks like I have a million and a half phone calls to make so my girls aren't disappointed."

"Good luck," Yvette said. "But don't forget to tell them to show up anyway and get their signed book."

"Oh, I will," she said with a definitive nod. "It was just easier when there was going to be some man-candy in the house." She smirked and grabbed a book with a bare-chested man on the cover. "Now I have to sell them on pastries and sexy werewolf shifters."

"Ms. Betty," Yvette said with a sigh. "You're... something else."

"I get that a lot," she said with a wink as she placed the book back on the shelf. "It's part of my charm. See you tomorrow." She swept from the store, moving faster than Yvette would've thought possible.

"She's got a bee in her bonnet," Brinn said.

"You can say that again."

Jacob poked his head out from behind the self-help aisle. "Is the coast clear?"

"Yes," Brinn and Yvette said at the same time, both of them laughing. He'd high-tailed it to the back of the store the moment they'd spotted Ms. Betty peering in the front window. Jacob had claimed he had paperwork to complete before he left town for the weekend, but Yvette knew better.

They'd gone through the books together two days ago and worked out their next order. There wasn't anything left to do, unless he'd been working up a new business plan that he hadn't told her about. He'd just been too much of a coward to risk hanging out with Ms. Betty. Yvette couldn't blame him, though. She wouldn't want to subject herself to so much blatant objectification either.

"Are you ready to go?" she asked him.

"Yep."

Yvette turned to Brinn. "We're headed out to get dinner. If for some reason Miranda calls or shows up early tonight, text me. I can be here in five minutes."

"Got it. See you in the morning." She turned her attention to Jacob. "Have a nice trip. And try not to gloat too much about the fabulous weather L.A. is having."

"No promises," he said as he ushered Yvette out of the store and into his truck. But instead of heading to the other end of Main Street to Woodlines, he steered his truck onto a residential street that turned into one of the many mountain roads that surrounded the valley of Keating Hollow.

"Please tell me you're not going to turn out to be an ax murderer," she said as she glanced over the ridge, eyeing the town.

"Ax murderer? No. That wouldn't be my weapon of choice," he said with a grin.

"Funny."

The road became narrower and more winding the further they drove, and just when she was sure he was taking her all the way to the top of the mountain, he turned down a hidden driveway and stopped in front of a beautiful, modern house with large floor-to-ceiling windows.

"Whoa," she said. "You *live* here?"

"That's the rumor." He jumped out of his truck that was nowhere near as nice as the home nestled into the side of the mountain and met her at the steps that led to his front door. "I thought it might be nice to have a home-cooked meal."

Since their Tuesday night at Woodlines, grabbing food after work together had become a habit. Each afternoon, they'd been busy canvasing the area with flyers for the signing and while they were out, they'd grabbed dinner. So the fact that he was bringing her back to his place meant he'd actually planned something.

It also meant this was looking a lot like a date. She should've said something. Should've called him on it, but she didn't. She didn't even want to. She liked him too much and wanted an evening with him before he left town.

Once they were inside, Yvette turned and sucked in a gasp as she stared out over the redwood-covered valley. The sun had already set, but the night was clear enough that she could see the lights from Keating Hollow below them as well as the silver moon bouncing off the river. "This is… something else, Jacob."

"It's better now that you're here."

She turned and smirked at him. "Nice line."

"It's the truth." He grabbed her hand and tugged her over to the gleaming white kitchen. Everything was modern and brand new, and the home suited him perfectly. He poured them each a glass of wine, and as he handed her one, he added, "But you should really see it in the morning. On rare days, you can see all the way to the Pacific."

"Are you trying to make some sort of suggestion, Jacob Burton?" she asked as she walked around the kitchen island to stand in front of him.

His dark eyes flashed with desire as he studied her. "If I was, would the answer be yes?"

Yes. The word was on the tip of her tongue. Instead she said, "Not tonight. I have a guest to host."

"Right. We'll save that for next week." He nodded to the table. "Have a seat. I'll be just a minute."

She raised her eyebrows in curiosity. "Did you manage to score some take out?"

He laughed. "Did you see any bags of food in the truck?"

"No."

"Well, there's your answer." Jacob opened his giant stainless steel fridge and produced two ahi tuna salads. "I hope you like fish."

"Love it."

"Good." He handed her a fork. "Dig in."

DINNER CONSISTED of ahi tuna salad, crab cakes, and then blackberry pie for dessert with plenty of whipped cream. Yvette had to give him credit. In the week they'd known each other, the man had definitely been paying attention. After dinner, they sat near Jacob's gas fireplace and talked about the weekend coming up. Actually, Yvette talked about the weekend, Jacob mostly listened.

"What about you? I know you said you needed to go home to settle some things with the business. Does that mean you'll have to see Sienna?" Yvette asked.

Jacob's good mood instantly soured, and he frowned. "Yes. She's insisting on seeing me before we finalize everything."

"Why?"

He shrugged. "No idea. It's been over a year since I last saw her. I imagine she wants to try to absolve herself of her sins, so to speak—try to get me to forgive her so she doesn't need to feel guilty or something."

Yvette took another sip of wine, hating the twinge of jealousy that suddenly appeared out of nowhere. "Do you forgive her?"

"Nope."

"Oh." She couldn't help but be curious about his breakup. She knew the basics. Sienna had taken off with his best friend just a few months before she and Jacob were to be married, but beyond that, she was short on details. Had they been happy?

Had he really loved her? Yvette couldn't imagine him promising to marry someone he didn't love with his whole heart. He was just that kind of guy. He put all he had into the things he cared about.

"Listen, can we talk about something else?" he asked. "I'm not trying to hide anything, but it's bad enough I have to deal with her tomorrow. I don't want her to spoil tonight, too."

"Absolutely." Yvette didn't want the ghost of his past ruining their night either. She reached for his hand and laced her fingers through his. "Tell me how you found this house. It's... well, it suits you perfectly."

He chuckled. "It should. I had it built."

She sat up, giving him her undivided attention. "What? When?"

"Last year." He drained the last of his wine and placed the glass on an end table. "You know my aunt lives here, right?"

"Of course. Everyone knows Miss Maple," she said.

"Yeah, I spent a few summers with her when I was a kid. And throughout my childhood, those summers were always my best memories. So after everything blew up, Keating Hollow was really the only place I wanted to be. After scouting the limited real estate options, I ended up buying this lot and hiring a contractor. I came up a few times during the process to check on it, but for the most part we did everything by phone or email." He waved his free hand around the room. "What do you think?"

"It's gorgeous. The house, the view, the finishing touches..." she sent him a flirty smile, "and the man who owns it."

"Gorgeous, huh? That's a big improvement over 'somewhat-decent.'" His dark eyes sparkled as he leaned in, clearly angling for a kiss. But before his lips could find hers, Yvette's phone dinged with a text.

She put her finger up, stopping him, and fished out her

phone. “It’s Miranda. She’s about ten minutes outside of town. Time to head back to reality.”

“Reality sucks,” he said, but he winked at her as he collected the wine glasses and took them to the kitchen.

“Couldn’t agree more.” She waited for him by the door then followed him out into the chilly night.

The minute they were back in the truck, Jacob’s fingers curled around hers, and he brought her hand up to his lips and gently kissed her knuckles. “I’m going to miss our dinners this weekend.”

Her heart fluttered a little at the tenderness in his tone. “Me, too. But you’ll be back on Monday, right?”

He nodded as he cranked the engine.

“Good. Come over to my place, and I’ll cook this time.”

“I like the sound of that,” he said. “Are you taking requests?”

“Do your requests have anything to do with food?” she asked.

He let out a hearty laugh. “No.”

“I didn’t think so. The answer is no. That way we’ll both be surprised.”

He glanced over at her, his smile wide. “It’s like you’ve known me for months instead of days. I like it. I like it very much.”

“Me too.” But she was acutely aware that she liked it too much. And she wasn’t sure what to do about that. So far, they’d just held hands, kissed, and flirted a lot. Under those circumstances, a botched romantic relationship could probably still be saved, but if they went any further… She just didn’t know.

It wasn’t long before Jacob pulled into her driveway alongside her Mustang. She’d picked it up from her father’s house earlier in the week, but thanks to Jacob chauffeuring her around, she hadn't had to use it once. Saturday would be a different story, and she knew she'd miss seeing him first thing.

She jumped out of the truck, and Jacob followed her up to her door, but instead of going in, she turned to him. "What are we going to do about this?"

"About what?" he asked hesitantly.

"This." She waved a hand between them. "You and me and this relationship we're building."

"Um, leave it where it is and see where it goes?" he asked, looking like a deer in headlights, no doubt from her use of the word 'relationship.'

"Relax," she said with a laugh. "I'm not trying to define anything or ask for some sort of commitment. I'm just… we're playing with fire here, and we both know it."

His sexy grin was back. "I know I'd like to play with a little fire."

"See." She pressed a hand to his chest. "This is what I'm talking about. How long do you think it's going to be before we end up crossing those relationship lines we set?"

His smile vanished, and his expression turned serious. "You know, Yvette, I don't think I can answer that. And neither can you. We can both say this is strictly business, but I think it's clear that's not really the case. The only real question is if we're brave enough to let it happen."

"Well, that was honest," she said, feeling a little overwhelmed.

"It's the only way I know how to be," he said as he brushed a lock of hair off her shoulder. "I don't know about you, but whatever this is that's happening, it's the easiest, most natural thing that I've ever felt. And while I both appreciate and share your concerns about the fact that we're business partners, I'm not certain I'm going to be able to walk away from this unless you're just not interested. Tell me you're not, Yvette, and I'll leave you alone."

Her throat went dry as she shook her head. She swallowed hard then said, "I can't tell you that. It wouldn't be true."

"There, see? We both told the truth. How about we just say that we'll both keep being honest with each other. I want to see this through, and I think you do too. Can we make a pact that the moment either of us loses interest, we just say so? I think as long as we communicate with each other, anything is possible."

He was living in Fantasyland. She was sure of it. None of her romantic relationships had ended in friendship. But still, she nodded. At the age of thirty-two it was time to grow up a little. If he could handle it, she could. "Okay, I'm in." She offered him her hand to shake on the deal, but he shook his head and kissed her instead—a toe-curling, *don't you dare forget about me while I'm gone this weekend* kind of kiss.

When he finally let her go, her knees had turned to rubber, and she was completely out of breath.

Someone started to clap and yelled out, "Whoo hoo. That was some performance. I give it a perfect ten!"

Yvette and Jacob both turned and spotted a woman wearing a black-lace corset dress, knee-high, lace-up boots, and silver bangles that covered her entire left forearm.

"I told that airheaded Sienna she was making a huge mistake," she said as she approached Jacob. "Can you imagine Brian kissing anyone like that?" she asked him.

Jacob let out a startled laugh and said, "Honestly, Miranda, that isn't anything I want to think about or have lodged in my brain. But thanks for the compliment."

"You're welcome." Then she turned to Yvette. "Hi, I'm Miranda. You must be Yvette."

Yvette collected herself enough to offer her hand to the

author, but Miranda brushed it aside and flung her arms around Yvette.

"I'm a hugger," Miranda said into Yvette's ear. "It's nice to meet you."

"You, too," Yvette said.

She let go, grabbed her small overnight bag, and linked arms with Jacob. "Show me inside. I'm freezing out here."

"You got it," he said. "Need help with anymore luggage?"

"Yep. It's in the trunk." She glanced over her shoulder at Yvette. "Will you be a doll and unload it for me?"

"Sure." Yvette unlocked her door for Jacob and Miranda then retreated to the woman's sleek black Mercedes. The trunk was already popped open and when Yvette opened the lid, she groaned. It was packed tight, with no room to spare. Surely she hadn't brought all that stuff for her two-night stay in Keating Hollow, had she?

Yvette ran into the house and found them in the living room. Miranda was sitting on Jacob's lap, already regaling him with a story from her last trip to Paris.

"There was this gorgeous waiter at the neighborhood café, and you know me," she said, patting his cheek. "I never can resist a pretty face."

Yvette cleared her throat. "Um, excuse me Miranda, but did you need everything in your trunk? Or was there a specific bag you wanted?"

"Oh, right." She wrinkled her nose as she contemplated. "It is a bit much, isn't it?" She ran a hand through her long black hair and sighed. "You know what? You better just bring it all in. I'm never sure just who I'm going to feel like being in the morning."

"Who you feel like being?" Jacob asked.

She shrugged. "I like options."

He patted her leg. "Then let me up. I'll help Yvette."

"You're such a gentleman," she said, her eyes twinkling. "Why is it we never spent the night together?"

"Because you were my fiancée's bridesmaid," he said as he grabbed her by the waist and removed her from his lap. "That would've been bad form."

"Right." She nodded. "And now you're dating Yvette here?" she asked.

"Not exactly," he said at the same time Yvette blurted out, "Yes, he is."

"Oh, now this is interesting," Miranda said, clapping her hands together. "I can't wait to see how this is going to turn out."

Yvette knew Miranda was waiting for some big blowup, for Yvette to get mad or Jacob to run as fast as he could. Instead, Jacob walked up to her and said, "So, we're officially dating."

"Yes. Get used to it."

He smiled. "I already am."

CHAPTER 12

"Yvette?" Miranda swept into the kitchen wearing a black satin-and-lace negligee, a matching robe, and fur-lined high-heeled slippers. The only splash of color she wore was the red polish on her toes.

"Yes?" Yvette took a sip of her cranberry spice tea and marveled at the woman's commitment to her fashion choices.

"Do you have any mascara remover? I seem to have forgotten mine."

Yvette nearly choked on her tea as she held back a laugh. The woman had actually forgotten something? She'd packed four suitcases, an overnight bag, and two totes. Yvette cleared her throat. "I believe so. I'll be right back."

"Thanks." Miranda glided over to the tea pot and said, "Is there more?"

She nodded. "Help yourself." When Yvette returned, she found Miranda sitting at the table with her feet up on one of the chairs and a cup of tea in front of her. She handed the author the makeup remover. "Here you go."

"Thank you." The woman batted her mascara-laden

eyelashes and waved at her face. "This was going to be a major mess."

Yvette sat across from her. "I can see how that would be a problem."

Miranda took a long sip of tea as she eyed Yvette. Then she put her cup down and leaned forward, watching Yvette intently. "He's fragile, you know."

"Who?" Yvette asked, surprised. "Jacob?"

"Yes. Has he told you what happened?"

"Some," Yvette said, uncomfortable with the conversation. She didn't know this woman. Nor did she know how close she was to Jacob. He'd gotten her number easily, but it wasn't as if he'd had her in his contacts. Besides, whatever relationship Yvette and Jacob were starting, she was certain he wouldn't appreciate anyone butting in, much less one of his ex's friends who was close enough to have been one of her bridesmaids.

"So you know he was heartbroken," she said, leaning back. "And betrayed."

Betrayed, yes. She'd known that. Heartbroken? Yvette hadn't gotten that impression. Not specifically anyway. Angry, hurt, and jaded, yes. But she hadn't considered he might have been devastated by Sienna's betrayal. "I don't think Jacob would want us talking about this."

Miranda let out a humorless snort. "I'm certain he wouldn't. But that's not going to stop me. I'm his guardian angel, you know."

Yvette raised her eyebrows. "You are?"

"Oh, yes. He's been on my project list since before he met Sienna. I told him she wasn't the one, but he didn't believe me."

Miranda was so serious, Yvette couldn't help but wonder if the writer actually believed that guardian angels were real or if she just thought herself a gifted matchmaker. Yvette stared at her, not sure what to make of the eccentric woman. "Why are you telling me this?"

"Because, Yvette, it's obvious he's smitten with you, and I want to make sure you're not going to stomp all over his heart the way Sienna did."

It was Yvette's turn to let out a snort. "I assure you, his heart has nothing to fear from me. In fact, I'm fairly certain *I'm* the one in danger here."

Miranda's expression softened, and she covered Yvette's hand with her own. Light reflected off the impressive collection of silver rings on her fingers as she squeezed lightly. "You care for him."

Of course she did. "We just started dating," she said lamely.

Miranda chuckled softly. "From my perspective, it looks a lot more serious than that. Listen, I already made one mistake when it comes to Jacob. I can't afford to do it again. I don't want to lose my wings." She winked. "Angels only get so many chances, you know."

"Um, okay," Yvette said, suddenly wondering if it was safe to have someone who seemed not quite right in the mind staying at her house.

"It's probably best that you know Jacob's the only reason I decided to do this signing on such short notice. No offense to you, of course."

"None taken." Yvette had been surprised when the author had said yes to such a last-minute request. But now that she knew Miranda thought she was some sort of steward for Jacob's love life, it made more sense.

"I had a feeling he'd met someone. When I spoke to him, I could just sense it in his energy. So here I am!" She raised her arms in the air as if she were showing herself off.

"Here you are," Yvette echoed half-heartedly.

"And I needed to see for myself if he'd chosen wisely this time."

Yvette gritted her teeth, hating that she was clearly being judged. "This is really none of your business. Like I said, Jacob and I just started seeing each other."

"I know." Her expression turned serious as she peered at Yvette. "All I'm trying to say is that I know Jacob comes off as an incredible flirt with lots of self-confidence, but there's a whole lot more to him than that. Don't mistake him for just another guy who's only interested in having a good time. There's a huge heart underneath it all, and he deserves someone great. Someone who isn't afraid of his baggage."

What baggage? A crazy ex? Yvette could relate. She had one of her own. Or at least Isaac had been acting crazy lately. Yvette opened her mouth then closed it, not at all sure what she should say to this woman. Finally, she decided Miranda was just being a protective friend and said, "We all have baggage, Miranda. Trust me. That doesn't scare me. But I think you're worrying prematurely. Jacob and I have only known each other a week."

"Sometimes that's all it takes, Yvette," she said with a small smile. Then she uncurled from her chair and floated upstairs.

It was a long time before Yvette got to sleep that night. And when she did, she dreamed of Jacob and a tiny little girl with dark curls.

~

"Wow," Miranda said, peering out the window of the bookstore at the crowd. "Are they all witches?" She was all dressed up in a short purple-lace dress, striped stockings, and pointy black boots. To complete her witchy attire, she had an eye pendant tied around her neck and dark, shadowy eye makeup.

"No," Yvette said, thinking the woman was totally over the top in all the right ways. "Some of them, sure. But most of them are here just to be wowed by the festivities." All of the businesses along Main Street had pulled out all the stops for Keating Hollow's New Year Witch's Festival. The windows had been spelled to wow the tourists, and the witches inside were showing off their magical talents, all with the explicit goal of keeping the tourists happy and their wallets open.

The festival had been Noel's idea a few years back. January in Keating Hollow could be awfully slow and rough on the local economy. But now that tourists were making the town an annual January trip, all of the businesses had increased their first quarter bottom lines.

"Oh, look, people are already lining up for the signing," Miranda gasped. "Oh, my gosh. I'm so glad I said yes to this." She hurried back over to the table Yvette had set up for her and quickly started loading Miranda Moon bookmarks, pens, pentacle-shaped bottle openers, and other swag onto the table.

"I'm about to open," Brinn said. "Ready?"

"I think so," Miranda said. "Let's do this."

Brinn unlocked the door, and from ten a.m. until well past four o'clock, there was a steady stream of people who worked their way through Miranda's line and the bookstore itself. Miranda powered through it all with only two wardrobe changes. Just before noon, she'd changed into a Glenda the Good Witch-type outfit that was silver from head to toe. And then just past two in the afternoon, she'd changed again. Her final outfit consisted of a leather skirt and corset, with black fishnet stockings and spiked six-inch heels that had a spider-web look. She'd put her hair into a high ponytail and braided it, making her look like a serious badass.

"And that's the last Miranda Moon book," the author said, standing up and grinning from ear to ear. She held up her hand and stretched her fingers as if working out the kinks. "That's gonna hurt tomorrow. I don't think I've ever signed so many books."

"They're gone?" Yvette gasped out. "You're kidding. All of them?"

"All of them. Unless you have some hiding in the back," she said.

Yvette shook her head. She'd personally moved all the books out onto the floor the day before, figuring she'd get Miranda to sign the leftovers so she could advertise them online. "Whoa."

"Whoa is right!" A woman with long platinum-blond hair said as she scooted behind the table and held her arms open for Miranda. She was dressed all in white and floated like an angel.

"Kasey!" Miranda said with a squeal. "You made it!"

The two wrapped their arms around each other and rocked back and forth with excitement. When they broke apart, Kasey said, "You killed it, girl. My goddess, I can't believe you moved that many books."

Miranda narrowed her eyes. "How do you know how many I moved? Did you sneak in here earlier and not say hi to me?"

"Guilty!" She grinned. "The line was so long, we decided to head out for lunch at that great brewery just down the street." Kasey waved to two other women. One was short and round with stylish gray hair, while the other had dark skin and beautiful, tight dark curls. Both of them were dressed in jeans, fur-lined boots, and warm sweaters. Clearly, Miranda and Kasey were the fashionistas of the group, while their two friends were happy to blend into the background.

"All three of you are here!" Miranda ran over to the other two women and gave each of them a quick hug. Grinning, she turned to Yvette and said, "Yvette, these are my three besties, Kasey Willis, Leann Viking, and Georgia Exler. They're all writers as well."

"Well, hello there." Yvette offered her hand to each of the women. Once Miranda had introduced them, Yvette knew instantly who they were and what they wrote. "It's such a pleasure to have a store full of such talented paranormal romance writers. Welcome to Hollow Books."

"I just adore that window display," Kasey said. "Any chance we can work something out for my next release?"

"Absolutely," Yvette said. "Interested in doing a signing?"

Kasey's grin widened. "You bet I am. So are my girls here." She waved to Leann and Georgia. "We could do a group one or..."

"Let's go into my office and take a look at the schedule," Yvette said. She turned to Miranda. "Do you need anything? Something to drink? A snack?"

"Brinn's already taking care of it." Miranda waved at her three friends and then turned her attention to a couple of teenagers who were clutching worn copies of her earlier books.

"Look, Miranda has fangirls," Kasey said.

"The paranormal genre is hugely popular around here," Yvette said. "Probably for obvious reasons."

"I should say so," Leann said, patting her gray curls. "And that's why all three of us came to check out your bookstore. I have to be honest, the store itself left a little to be desired."

Yvette's eyebrows shot up as she tried her best to not scowl at the woman. How could anyone not adore the old Victorian cottage? The moment Yvette had stepped foot into the place, she'd instantly fallen in love with the wood floors, the built-in bookcases, and the gorgeous crown moldings. "Really? What is it you think would make it better?"

"A display of my books would go a long way in sprucing up the place." Leann grinned and gave Yvette a teasing smile. "Actually, the place is lovely, and I'm jealous as a hell cat of Miranda right now."

The other two authors laughed at their friend, and Yvette chuckled as she led them into her office. "I see. Well, let's change that."

"Really?" Leann asked. "Just like that?"

"Just like that," Yvette said. "We're already scheduling more events. What I'd like to do is feature your next release and have you come do a signing during one of the town's many festivals. What do you think?"

"Yes," the three authors said in unison.

Yvette's stomach did a little flip. All three of the authors sitting across from her had large audiences, and she knew she was onto something big for their store. She flipped her calendar open, grabbed a pen, and said, "Excellent. Let's get all three of you on the schedule."

CHAPTER 13

Norm's assistant opened the door to the plush office and waved Jacob in. "Norm will be right with you."

"Thanks, Penny." He strode across the office and stopped at the floor-to-ceiling window, looking out over the city. Off in the distance, the sun bounced off the brilliant blue Pacific Ocean. There'd been a time in his life when he'd loved southern California. The sun, the surf, the whirlwind business opportunities, it'd all made his blood hum. Now he felt nothing.

All he wanted to do was head back to his house on the hill, to where the fog rolled off the northern coast over the redwoods. He'd only been living in Keating Hollow for about two weeks, but he'd been making the mental shift for over a year. The small town was starting to weave its way into his being… or was it Yvette that was taking hold of him? He saw her face swimming in his mind, and it became clear to him that L.A. was his past, not his future.

"Jacob," Norm said jovially as he swept into the office. "You're right on time just like always."

"I try." Jacob strode over to his family friend and attorney, holding his hand out.

Norm took Jacob's hand with both of his and shook it warmly. "How was the trip down?"

Jacob shrugged. "Fine. Do you know what this is about? I thought the paperwork was already in order."

Norm frowned. "Unfortunately, no. Ms. Teller just said that she needed to speak to you in person before she'd sign anything. Presumably, she'll be ready to finalize everything once she's had a chance to meet with you."

"Right." Jacob ran a hand through his dark hair, not believing for a minute that the day would end with him finally being free of his ex. But he had to try. He was more than ready to move on. "When will she be here?"

"She's already in the conference room down the hall," Norm said. "She's ready when you are."

Jacob took a deep breath and nodded. "Fine. Let's get this over with."

"All right. Just remember that if she tries to change the terms of either agreement, do not commit to anything. Just tell her you'll need to run it by your lawyer. Got it?"

He let out a snort of derision and in an unmistakably bitter tone, he said, "Why would she change anything? She's getting everything she wants."

"Except you," Norm said.

"She doesn't want me. Trust me on that one." Jacob squared his shoulders. "Don't worry, Norm. I won't promise her anything past what we've already worked out."

"Good. Let's go."

Jacob followed his lawyer to the corner conference room. The moment they walked in, he heard her suck in a small gasp. He turned his gaze on Sienna and wondered how he'd ever thought her the most beautiful woman in the world. There was no denying she was attractive. Her long dark hair was as sleek and shiny as ever. Her makeup was flawless, as was her designer-label, perfectly tailored pantsuit.

Sienna's lawyer stood and walked over to Norm. "Ms. Teller would like a moment alone with Mr. Burton before we move forward on the settlement."

Norm glanced at his client. "Is that all right with you, Jacob?"

He gave his lawyer a half shrug. It was no less than he'd expected. She wouldn't want the lawyers listening in on whatever BS she would try to lay on him. "I guess."

"Thank you, Jacob," she said from her spot behind the big conference table.

He didn't answer her.

"I'll be right outside," Norm said and followed the other lawyer out into the hall.

Jacob turned his gaze to his ex-fiancée. "What is this all about?"

Her bottom lip trembled as she stared up at him. "I thought..." She blew out a breath. "I think we need to clear the air."

Jacob shook his head. "What happened is ancient history, Sienna. All I want is to sell the house and get untangled from your business. Any—"

"Our business," she said faintly.

"Our business?" he echoed. "You've got to be kidding me. Enchanted Bliss was never mine. You didn't take one suggestion I made, didn't ask my opinion on anything. All you wanted was for me to write the checks. Well, you got what you wanted. It's yours. And all you have to do is start paying off the investment capital, *interest free,* within one year of making a profit. You got your dream funded, my best friend, and half the appreciation on the house *I bought* for us. What more do you want from me?"

She stared down at the folder on the table, and Jacob started to wonder if she'd finally found her conscience. "Nothing, Jacob," she said, her voice wobbly. "I don't want anything from you."

He clenched his hands into fists and had to hold back the strong desire to punch something. "Then what are we doing here, Sienna?"

"I..." She glanced away, her face pale.

He moved closer, clutching the back of one of the chairs as he really studied her for the first time since walking into the room. Beneath the heavy layer of makeup, he noted the dark circles under her eyes and a new worry line creasing her forehead. Her eyes were tired, and her complexion was pasty, despite her efforts to disguise it. "Sienna?" he asked, suddenly worried. "Are you sick?"

She glanced up at him, tears in her eyes as she shook her head. "No."

Alarm made his heart start to race. Either she was lying, or something else was seriously wrong. He'd seen Sienna cry before. She didn't hesitate to use tears as a weapon when it came to getting what she wanted. But he didn't think that was the case in this instance. He'd seen that little act of hers enough times to know that this situation was different. Whatever was going on with her, she was really upset.

Jacob walked around to her side of the table and pulled out one of the chairs. He sat, leaning forward as he held her teary gaze. "What is it, Si? What's happened?"

The tears were coming faster now as she shook her head and desperately tried to wipe them away. "I'm sorry. This isn't... you don't deserve this."

She was right. He didn't. But he had cared for her once, and he couldn't just walk away while she was so obviously upset. He took one of her hands gently in his own. "Whatever it is, you know you can trust me. I'm here."

She gave him a watery smile and choked out, "Only because I forced your hand."

"That doesn't matter now. You obviously had your reasons. Why don't you just tell me what you came here to say? I'm not going anywhere until you do."

She glanced down at the folder in front of her then back at him. "I um… I owe you an explanation."

Sienna owed him a lot more than that, but he'd let all of that go months ago. "That doesn't matter anymore. I just want to move past this, Sienna."

"I know." She nodded and pulled her hand away from him. Grabbing her sleek black handbag that was on the table, she started to rummage around. She found a tissue, and as she dabbed at her now-swollen eyes, she said, "You need to know why I left."

He opened his mouth to protest, but she held a hand up, stopping him. "Please, Jacob, I need to get this out."

"Okay." He sat back in his chair, watching as she got to her feet and stared out of the window. It was then he noticed she looked different. Her body had changed. She was no longer the rail thin, super model type but was now rounder, softer looking. The manufactured beauty had been replaced with something real and accessible. "You look… different," he said before he could stop himself.

She turned to eye him warily. "Good or bad different?"

"Good different. More…" He wanted to say human, but that sounded harsh even to his own ears.

"More what, Jacob?" she asked, tilting her head to one side with a curious expression.

"I don't know… authentic, I guess? Like you've settled into your own skin."

Emotion flickered in her eyes before she closed them and said, "A year can really change a person."

"I suppose so," he said. Then he narrowed his eyes. "How have you changed, Sienna?"

She bit down on her bottom lip and pressed one hand to her abdomen.

Jacob was done talking, and he was determined to wait for her to finally find the courage to tell him why he'd been summoned from Keating Hollow.

The minute hand clicked over on the wall clock, the sound almost deafening in the silence.

Finally, she turned her back to him and stared out at the city as she said, "I never wanted to hurt you."

He stifled an irritated sigh. "Isn't that what everyone says after they've hurt someone?"

"Yeah." She nodded, still facing the window. "I could've just stayed." She glanced over her shoulder. "My mom told me to, you know."

"I'm not surprised," Jacob said. Janice Teller loved the idea of her only daughter marrying into the Burton family. She'd told Jacob once that she always knew her daughter had the potential to marry well. Jacob had been offended on his fiancée's behalf. Sienna Teller didn't need to *marry well*. She was a college graduate who was intelligent enough to excel at whatever she put her mind to. In other words, she sure as heck didn't need Jacob or his family's money to make her mark on the world. "Has Brian won her over yet?"

She turned and faced him, her hands clasped in front of her. "I don't want to talk about Brian right now."

"Why not?" Jacob snapped. "He's the reason we're in this predicament."

"No, he isn't!" she shouted. "I am. Don't you get it yet, Jacob?"

He stood, his entire body vibrating with white-hot anger. "I get it, Sienna. You used me and ran off with my best friend, leaving me looking like a fool."

Her face paled again, and she shook her head. "I never meant for any of this to happen."

"You've said that before." He stalked to the other end of the room, needing to put as much distance between them as possible. "Just say whatever it is you need to say, Sienna. Whatever it is, I'm sure it isn't going to change anything between us."

"Trust me, Jacob. It changes everything," she said, her voice strong and full of certainty.

He turned to her, his insides cold as he stared her down.

She lifted her chin and said, "The reason I left was because I was pregnant."

Jacob blinked, wondering if he'd heard her correctly. Then his gaze dropped to her waist as if he was looking for evidence. There wasn't anything to see of course. She'd left over a year ago. If she'd kept the child, it would have been born months ago.

Child.

The word rolled around in his head. His child? Or Brian's? A cold chill washed over him. He cleared his throat. "Did you keep it?"

She jerked back as if he'd slapped her. "Of course I kept it. You know how much I wanted to have children."

"I also thought you wanted to marry me, but that didn't happen did it?" It was a petty thing to say, but the words had just flown out of his mouth.

Sienna gritted her teeth. When she spoke again, her voice

was low and barely audible. "How many more times do you want me to apologize?"

He sighed heavily. "I don't want you to apologize. I want you to sign the agreements so I can get on with my life."

"That's just it, Jacob. You can't get on with your life. Not the way you think," she said.

"And why not? You have Enchanted Bliss, Brian, and a child..." His voice trailed off on the word child. Hadn't she just said she'd left because she was pregnant? They'd been together, sleeping together, right up until she'd pulled the rug out from under him. His heart sped up, and suddenly the room started to spin. "Are you saying that your child could be mine?"

She stared at him for a few beats then nodded. "Jacob, I'm sorry I didn't tell you sooner—"

"I have a child?" he bellowed, completely beside himself with her betrayal. "You were pregnant with my child and you never told me?"

"I didn't know—"

"Of course you knew! You said you left because you were pregnant. Dammit, Sienna. I deserved to know. I should've been there through the pregnancy. I should've been there in the delivery room. How could you keep this to yourself? How?"

Her face flushed red, and she tilted her head down, staring at her clasped hands. "I'm so sorry, Jacob."

"I don't need your apologies, Sienna. I never did. All I needed was honesty." He stared at her, his insides hollowed out, and he realized that he felt absolutely nothing for his child's mother. Sadness washed over him. What a complete and utter mess. All he'd ever wanted was a wife to love, spoil, and call his partner. And someday a family to call his own. Eighteen months ago, he'd thought he had everything he'd ever wanted. The woman standing in front of him had stolen it all, including his child.

"I..." She clutched her throat with one hand. "I didn't know. I thought... I'd been with Brian for two months by then. You were off doing work for Bayside Books, and we'd barely seen each other. I thought for sure the baby was Brian's. When I told him, he confessed he'd always loved me. And I—um, I guess I'd always felt the same way. You know, he was with someone else when we first got together. I thought they'd get married, so I moved on with you. I loved you. I did, Jacob. I—"

He glared at her. "I don't want to hear it," he said flatly. "The last thing I want to hear is the details of your affair. All I care about in this moment is how you know this child is mine if you were so convinced Brian was the father."

"Brian kept saying she looks like you, and he demanded a blood test."

"She?" he asked on a hushed whisper, feeling as if his heart were going to explode.

"She." Sienna smiled softly then added, "Her name is Skye."

"Skye," he said just to hear the name on his lips. He closed his eyes and tried to imagine what she might look like. But before he got too invested, he had to know for sure Skye was his. "What did the blood test say?"

"Her blood type is B. Both Brian and I are O." Her expression turned sad. "The doctor said there is no way she could be Brian's."

Jacob's breath left him as reality crashed down on him. *B.* His blood type was B. Unless Sienna had been sleeping with a third person, Skye was definitely his child. He hated to ask and definitely didn't want to know the answer, but he had no choice. "Was there anyone else?"

She frowned. "What do you mean?"

"I mean did you sleep with anyone else besides me or Brian? Is there any chance at all Skye isn't mine?"

"Jeez, Jacob. No. Of course not. Why would you even ask that?"

He gave her a flat stare. "Hmm, I wonder why, Sienna."

She opened her mouth to no doubt argue with him, but she quickly shut it and inclined her head so that she was staring at her feet. "I guess I deserved that."

He couldn't disagree. Still, whatever she'd done, it didn't matter now. Jacob had just learned he had a daughter. He walked over to her, and very gently lifted her chin with two fingers so that he could look her in the eye. "When can I see her?"

CHAPTER 14

Monday morning rolled around dark and dreary, but Yvette found herself dancing around her office, her fist in the air as she celebrated the weekend's numbers. She'd just finished adding up the sales they'd raked in during the signing and was elated to find out they were on track to have the best month ever. She couldn't wait until Jacob came in so she could share the good news.

Just the thought of seeing his face after he'd been gone all weekend made her stomach do a little flip. And even though she was pretty certain Miranda had been off her rocker with the guardian angel stuff, Yvette hoped she'd been right when she'd said Jacob was smitten, because it was clear Yvette was head over heels for him.

The bell on the front door chimed, and Yvette hurried out into the shop, expecting to see Jacob. They still had ten minutes until they opened, and Brinn had the day off. But instead of her tall, dark, and handsome business partner, she found Hanna Pelsh at the pastry and coffee bar, stocking the display with fresh cookies.

"Hanna! You don't have to do that." Yvette hurried over and nudged her friend out of the way. "You're already doing me a huge favor by delivering this stuff. You don't have to put it away as well."

Hanna shrugged. "I wasn't sure you were here yet."

Yvette had given the Pelshes a key to the front door as part of the delivery arrangement so they could have a bigger window of time for deliveries. Since Brinn was off, no one had been upfront when Hanna had let herself in. "Thank you. You're so thoughtful, but I can take it from here."

"Sure." Hanna stepped out from behind the café counter and glanced around. "I can't believe you got this place in order already. I heard you guys were busier than the brewery this weekend."

Yvette grinned. "That was Saturday. We still had a good crowd yesterday, but man, that signing was crazy successful. Be prepared. We'll be doubling our pastry order for next month's signing."

"Excellent. I'll let my mom know." She moved to the door. "Tell Jacob and Brinn hi for me."

"Will do."

The bell on the door chimed as she let herself out, and Yvette found herself wandering the store and wondering what she should do with herself. Brinn had stayed late the day before, and they'd managed to get the store back in order in record time. And because Yvette had known she'd be working the store by herself until Jacob showed up, she'd come in early to deal with the bookkeeping.

Now she found herself by the front door, eyeing the deserted street, looking for Jacob's familiar truck. When she didn't even see any lights shining through the rain, she sighed, flipped the open sign and headed for the café counter.

Armed with a fresh latte and a couple of cookies, Yvette

positioned herself behind the checkout counter and cracked open Jovee Winters' newest twisted fairy tales book.

YVETTE PICKED up her smart phone and sighed. No calls. It was late afternoon, and the weather had only continued to deteriorate. Thunder rumbled overhead, and the rain had become a punishing downpour over Keating Hollow. She'd expected Jacob sometime before noon, but so far, she hadn't seen or heard from him. And after sending him two unanswered messages, she was getting worried.

The bookstore phone rang, and Yvette pounced. "Hollow Books, Yvette speaking."

"Hey, it's me," her sister Noel said.

Disappointment settled in her chest, and she sank down onto the stool behind the counter. "What's up, sis?"

"Faith is here. We wondered if you'd want to join us for dinner. I made pie."

"Pie for dinner?" Yvette asked.

"Yep. Blackberry. Whipped cream is in the fridge."

Yvette sat up straight on full alert. "What's wrong?"

"Nothing. Faith met someone." Noel's voice was full of mischief now.

Yvette glanced at the clock. "I'll be there in twenty minutes."

"Excellent."

The line went dead. Yvette replaced the phone on the charging station, grateful for the distraction. Now she wouldn't be sitting at home waiting for Jacob to call. She quickly cleaned the café station that had only been used twice that day then cashed out the register. After she took one last glance around the shop, she bundled up in her wool coat and hat and then locked up.

The biting wind cut right through her jeans and coat, while the rain blew in horizontal sheets. Normally Yvette would just walk down to her sister's inn, but tonight, she jumped in her Mustang and drove the two blocks. Still, by the time she made it from the parking space out in front of the Keating Hollow Inn and into the lobby, she was dripping and in desperate need of a hot cup of coffee.

"Noel?" she called as she slipped behind the check-in counter.

The door to Noel's apartment was flung open and Faith, her baby sister, stood in the doorway. She was gorgeous, with interesting, angular features and big green eyes. Yvette had always thought Faith had been made for the runways of Paris, but she'd been content to stay right there in Keating Hollow, working odd jobs while she completed her massage therapy schooling. She was holding two large mugs. Steam billowed out of the one in her left hand, and she thrust it at Yvette. "Here. You need this."

The scent of Irish whiskey assaulted her nose as she tilted the cup to her lips and took a long, fortifying sip. "Oh, thank you. You're a goddess."

"It's about time you noticed," Faith said and pulled Yvette into Noel's apartment.

Yvette glanced around at the tidy living room and spotted Noel lounging on the couch, her feet curled under her and a blanket wrapped around her shoulders. Her hair had been dyed and cut again. It was shoulder-length now with long layers and was a fetching strawberry blond that perfectly complemented her skin tone. Of the four sisters, Noel was the one who was always changing her look. "I'm here," Yvette said. "Where's the pie?"

Noel laughed. "In the kitchen. Are you starving?"

"Yes. I didn't get lunch today."

"Why not?" Noel frowned. "You couldn't have been that busy at the bookstore. Keating Hollow has been a ghost town since the storm rolled in."

"No, definitely not busy," Yvette said. "I just didn't have any help today, so I skipped lunch. It was Brinn's day off."

"What about Jacob? Wasn't he there?" Faith asked, flopping down onto the couch next to Noel.

"No. He's still out of town, I guess." Yvette sat in one of the arm chairs and glanced around. "Where are Olive, Daisy and Drew?"

"Olive is with her grandmother for the night, and Daisy and Drew are out on a father-daughter type date," Noel said, her eyes going soft. "Oh. Em. Gee." She pressed her hand to her heart. "You guys, this nearly killed me. This morning Daisy and I were in the kitchen getting breakfast ready when Drew walked in. We said our good mornings, and suddenly out of the blue, Daisy asked if she could take Drew out for dinner and a movie."

"Whoa, Noel. Looks like Daisy is moving in on your man," Yvette said with an exaggerated wink.

"It's true," Noel said soberly. "Those two... sometimes I swear the only reason Drew and I ended up together is because he fell in love with her."

Faith put her mug on the coffee table and turned to stare Noel in the eye. "Would you have it any other way?"

"Absolutely not," she said with a grin. "But dang... when does this girl get dinner and a movie?"

"Have you asked him?" Yvette asked.

She shrugged, and Yvette took that as a no.

Yvette laughed. "Your kid has a thousand percent more game than you do. Maybe you should take notes."

"Maybe," Noel grumbled, but the twitch of her lips gave her

away. "She's just got a cuteness that he can't resist. Do you know the last time he's told her *no* to anything at all?"

"When?" Faith asked, now perched on the edge of the couch.

"Never." Noel stood, leaving her mug on the table. "I'll be right out with the pie. Double heaping of whipped cream for everyone?" she asked, directing her question to Yvette.

"Yes for me," Yvette said and added, "Faith?"

But before their baby sister could answer, Noel laughed and said, "Everyone except for Faith. She has a man to impress."

"Impress, ha! We'll just see about that," Faith said, flinging her long blond hair over one shoulder with plenty of attitude. "He's the one who's going to need to impress me."

"Okay, hold on," Yvette said. "Who is this man, and where did you meet him?"

"Wait right there." Noel held her hand up. "This calls for pie first." She turned to Faith. "Do not say a word until I get back with the pie."

"Only if I get extra whip. These hips can handle it." Faith waved a hand over her long and lean body.

"No kidding," Yvette muttered under her breath. "I don't think I've looked like that since the sixth grade."

"We can't all be curvy, delicious pinups, now can we?" Faith shot back, giving her sister as good as she got.

Yvette grinned at her. "I guess we all have our own crosses to bear."

"Okay, enough, you two." Noel turned to Faith and pointed a finger at Yvette. "Do not let this one needle any information out of you, or I'll throw both of your pieces of pie out."

"I wouldn't dream of it," Faith said, leaning back into the couch cushions.

Yvette's mouth dropped open as she stared at Noel. "That's just rude. Pie is sacred."

"So is gossip about Keating Hollow's newest resident." She smirked and hurried into the kitchen.

Yvette snapped her attention to her younger sister as her pulse sped up. "Was she talking about Jacob?" As far as Yvette knew, Jacob was the new kid in town.

Faith shook her head. "Nope. She's talking about the contractor I hired for the spa. But let's wait until she gets back. You know she wasn't kidding about denying us the pie."

"You have a contractor already and there's something going on?" Yvette asked, ignoring the directive from her sister to cease gossip until the pie was in hand. She had every confidence she could take Noel if she tried to make good on her threat.

"What! No. Of course there isn't anything going on." Faith shook her head, but not before Yvette noticed the glimmer in her eyes.

"Oh, boy," Yvette said and sucked in a breath. "You've got it bad."

"Please. I just met the man." Faith rolled her eyes. "I know *you* like to work fast, but I like taking my time and enjoying the scenery a little... if you know what I mean."

Yvette sighed. She knew exactly what her sister meant. Her relationship with Jacob was new and fast and a lot overwhelming. And now she found herself in the awkward position of not knowing where he was or what he was up to, and she wasn't at all sure she was justified in being worried or annoyed. Did she deserve an explanation as to where he was? She thought so, but after only a week of dating... She was certain most people wouldn't see it that way.

"Yeah, I think you're onto something there. There's a lot to be said for taking things slow," Yvette said, wishing she'd had that willpower when it came to Jacob. Instead, she'd already checked her damned phone three times since she'd sat down in her sister's place.

"Speaking of enjoying the scenery," Faith said. "Whoa. I saw Jacob this morning, and even covered up in four layers of clothing, that man is so hot it's a miracle he's not on fire."

"You saw Jacob?" she blurted. "Where?"

"Incantation Café. He'd just gotten in from L.A. and said he needed some fuel to get him up the hill, whatever that means."

"His house is nestled into the side of the mountain," Yvette supplied, feeling completely deflated. She'd been telling herself that he just hadn't made it back to town yet, but Faith had laid eyes on him early in the day. That meant he should've had time to call her back to at least let her know he was okay. But he hadn't. The pit in her stomach grew, and as Noel brought them the heaping plates of pie and whipped cream, Yvette's ire grew to match it with each passing moment. Jacob had made it back to town and had ignored her. *Why?*

"Okay, time to spill the beans, lil sis," Noel said, handing each of them a plate. "Tell us every sordid detail."

Faith grabbed a fork and dipped into the pie. Just before she shoved a mound of pie and whipped cream into her mouth, she said, "I sort of walked in on him while he was showering."

"What?" Yvette said, dropping her fork.

"Whose shower?" Noel asked, narrowing her eyes. "Not the one here, I hope?"

Faith shook her head. "No, not here. Jeez, Noel, what do you think I'm doing? Loitering around hotels and breaking into rooms in the hopes of catching a glimpse of some guy's junk?"

"If you didn't walk in on him in a hotel room, then where?" Yvette asked, her curiosity definitely piqued.

Faith put the pie down and pulled out a key. "My new spa building."

"What?" both sisters screamed and ran toward her with their arms outstretched. "I can't believe it," Yvette said, whispering in her ear. "You're really doing this."

"I am." Faith beamed. "There's only one problem, and we're working on it right now."

"And that problem is…?" Yvette asked.

"My contractor was living in my workspace, or at least sleeping there sometimes and using my shower *without* me," Faith said. "And that just won't do."

"He's really freakin' hot, Yvette," Noel chimed in. "If I didn't already have Drew, I'd have to fight her for him. He's that good looking."

"Good luck,' Faith said with a snort. "I've been working out. I think I can take you."

Noel sized her sister up and gave her a short nod. "You know, I believe you could. You keep your contractor, and I'll keep the deputy sheriff."

"Now that you've got that settled, I'm still waiting to hear about this shower thing," Yvette said.

"His thing is huge," Faith said, her eyes wide and her hands about a foot apart.

Yvette blinked. Then she started cracking up. "Good for you. Are you going to do anything about it?"

Faith's smile grew with mischief. "We'll see. *After* the spa work is done."

"I'll drink to that." Noel raised her wine glass. "To mixing business and pleasure after the job is done."

"Here, Here!" Faith and Yvette said in unison.

"Just try to date him with his clothes on first," Yvette added.

Faith snorted. "I'll do my best."

CHAPTER 15

Jacob parked his truck in front of Hollow Books and flipped the engine off. The morning was dark and surly just like it had been the day before, and it suited his mood perfectly. His meeting with Sienna on Saturday had completely thrown him for a loop. He'd run through every emotion under the sun, starting with wonder and ending in complete and total rage.

He still couldn't understand how Sienna hadn't even considered letting him know he could be Skye's father, and now he'd missed the first six months of her life. How had he not seen how incredibly selfish she was when they'd been together? In some moments, he wasn't sure if he was angrier with her or with himself for being so blind.

After the revelation, he'd demanded to see Skye, but Sienna had refused, saying that the baby was in Aspen with her mother and Brian, where they were getting ready to open another Enchanted Bliss. He'd been two seconds away from booking a flight, but Sienna had gone into mama bear mode and convinced him it was better for him to sit with the news for a few days. She'd told him to go home and get used to the idea and then next week she'd come to Keating Hollow to let him meet his daughter.

It wasn't the plan he'd wanted, but when Sienna had told him she wasn't interested in playing games anymore and then proved it by signing the settlement agreement, he'd had no choice but to give her the benefit of the doubt. What else was he going to do? Fly to Aspen in the middle of winter and go door to door until he found them? He could, but then he'd look like the crazy one in that scenario.

Instead, he'd spent Sunday hiking Echo Mountain, trying to fatigue his muscles enough that he'd exhaust his mind as well. It hadn't worked. He hadn't slept a wink the night before, and when he'd arrived in Keating Hollow on Monday morning, he'd had a raging headache. After washing down a couple of aspirin with a strong cup of coffee laced with a shot of whiskey, he'd gone straight to bed. When he'd woken late in the evening, the headache was gone, but his rage was just getting started. And while it hadn't been the best way to deal with the news of his daughter, he spent the night finishing off the whiskey bottle.

Now he was hungover and had to figure out how to face Yvette. He hadn't meant to ignore her calls specifically, he'd just turned his phone off with the intention of ignoring the world.

The front door opened, and Yvette walked over to the driver's side window of his truck. He quickly lowered the window. "What's going on?" he asked her.

"That's what I was about to ask you. Is everything all right?" Her pretty dark eyes were full of concern.

"Yeah," he said, biting back a wince as he straight-up lied to her. "I was just finishing a phone call, and then I was coming right in."

Her gaze darted around the truck, and he had no doubt she was looking for the phone that was still tucked away in his console. When she didn't find it, she just nodded and said, "Okay."

"I'll be right behind you," he said.

"Of course." Her tone was clipped with slight annoyance at his obvious dismissal. And he knew he was messing everything up as she turned and strode back into the shop.

He hung his head for a moment, took a deep breath, and told himself to suck it up and stop acting like a selfish jerk. It was obvious she'd been worried about him, and she didn't deserve to be treated as if her concern meant nothing. He just wasn't anywhere near ready to share anything about the daughter he hadn't even met yet.

Jacob scrounged around for his phone, turned it on, and scowled at the dozen messages waiting for him. They'd just have to wait. He needed to talk to Yvette.

The store was a warm and welcoming reprieve from the chilly January morning, and Jacob instantly felt a little better. There was a fire lit in the fireplace in the café area, and the aroma of freshly brewed coffee combined with that ever-present scent of paperback books made him feel more at home than his modern house on the hill ever had.

"Good morning," Brinn said from her spot near the front table where she was arranging a new shipment of books. It was the same table that had held the overstock of Miranda Moon books the week before.

"Good morning, Brinn." He frowned as he studied the table. It was full of the latest *New York Times* bestsellers. "What happened to the Miranda Moon books?"

She grinned. "Sold out. Can you believe it? The weekend was incredible. I know Yvette is dying to tell you all about it."

"Sold out?" He blinked. "How is that possible?" He'd figured they'd probably do well, but while Miranda was a popular author for her genre, she was hardly a household name.

"The festival was a huge hit this year, and people came from the surrounding towns," Brinn said. "We were exhausted by the time Sunday rolled around."

"I'd guess so," he said as he headed for the café. After pouring himself the largest cup of coffee he could find, he went in search of Yvette.

She was sitting at her desk, concentrating on the computer screen, wearing plastic black-rimmed glasses, and her long chestnut hair was twisted up into a bun with a pencil holding it in place. He leaned against the doorframe and just stared at her, imagining undoing that bun and running his fingers through her silky hair. She was gorgeous in an unassuming way. Classy and real and everything he'd never known he wanted.

"Are you going to come in?" she asked, leaning back in the chair.

"I was just admiring the view," he said easily, letting himself forget the weekend's events even if just for a moment or two. "You look incredible today."

"Really?" She raised one eyebrow, her eyes flashing with annoyance. "Meanwhile, you look like you've been partying all weekend and smell like it, too."

"What?" He raised his hand to his mouth and breathed into it, then sniffed. There was no denying the faint whiff of whiskey. He groaned.

"Fun weekend?" she asked.

"No. Quite the opposite actually." He grabbed one of the office chairs and sat across from her. "Listen, Yvette, I'm sorry I was a no-show yesterday. I should've called."

"Are you under the impression that I'm upset because you didn't come into work?" she asked coolly.

"Well..." He'd obviously stepped in something with his failed apology, he just wasn't exactly sure where to go from there. "I'm guessing you're annoyed because I didn't return your phone calls. Still, I'd told you I'd be in, so I should've at least let you know I couldn't make it."

"And why is that?" She crossed her arms over her chest and eyed him with suspicion. "Were you held up in L.A. or something? Did you have a nice visit with Sienna?"

Her mention of Sienna sent that now-familiar rush of rage straight to his gut, and he wanted to growl at her, to tell her whatever he'd been doing was none of her business. They were business partners and nothing more. But that wasn't right, was it? He wouldn't go so far as to call Yvette his girlfriend, but on Friday, they *had* made it official that they were dating. That meant at the minimum that Yvette was a friend and possibly something a heck of a lot more. Still, she didn't have a right to question him about what he was doing with his ex. He'd already told her he was there to finalize paperwork.

"As a matter of fact, no, I did not have a nice visit with Sienna," he ground out, trying to ignore the pain sluicing through him as he thought of the daughter he hadn't yet met. "But she did sign the documents, so at least I can say that business is settled."

Yvette's annoyance cleared and was suddenly replaced with concern. "So it's done. Are you okay?"

No. Not even close, he thought. But he knew what she meant. She was talking about what should've been the final nail in the coffin of his relationship with Sienna. And on that point, he was perfectly fine. He didn't care one whit about Enchanted Bliss, and he'd even made a little money on the sale of the beach house, even though he'd had to split the appreciation value with Sienna. "Yeah, I'm okay."

"You're sure?" she asked. "The day I signed my divorce

papers, I thought I was fine. Then I went home and ate an entire half gallon of ice cream before drinking a bottle of wine."

He forced a smile and leaned in. "It's been over for a very long time, Yvette. I came to terms with it months ago. I just wasn't feeling the best yesterday and ended up using a bit of whiskey to help me sleep."

"A bit? It's clogging your pores, Jacob."

He chuckled. "Sorry about that. It won't happen again."

She appeared skeptical but seemed to decide to take his explanation at face value rather than press the issue. "So, you didn't have the best weekend, but it's over and now you can move on."

"Right," he agreed, knowing there would be no moving on until he met his daughter and had legal custody rights. He hadn't discussed it with Sienna, but if she thought he was going to hang out in the background and be an absentee father, she was wildly mistaken.

"Do you want to hear about our weekend?" Yvette asked with a grin.

"Yes," he said, a smile coming easier now that they were done talking about his personal life. "I hear it was a resounding success."

"You have no idea." She sat up and clasped her hands together, excitement radiating from her like a beacon of light. "The place was a madhouse," she started. Then she launched into the details of the weekend and ended with, "We've already made more this month than any other month since the store opened. And I've already locked in three more authors for signings this year, plus have another three seriously interested. I think we're really on to something, don't you?"

He stared into her excited, sparkling eyes and wished with everything he had that he could sweep her up in his arms, swing her around the office, and plant a long, victorious kiss on her sweet mouth. But now that he knew about Skye, he couldn't continue to muddy the waters with her, couldn't enter a relationship he knew was doomed when he left Keating Hollow to move back to L.A. or Aspen or wherever Sienna took his daughter. Because one thing was for sure, wherever Skye was, he was going to follow.

"Definitely, Yvette. Your idea really paid off. Congratulations." He smiled warmly at her, happy to know that at the very least when he left town, Yvette wouldn't have to worry about losing Hollow Books. He'd already decided he'd become a silent partner and let her run it how she saw fit. It was obvious she was more than capable.

"Our idea," she said. Then she handed him the scheduling book and the up-to-date sales figures for the first half of the month.

He took one look at it and knew he was making the right decision. Given time, she'd turn Hollow Books into a premier independent bookstore, and he couldn't be prouder to be a part of it, even if he would soon be on the sidelines.

CHAPTER 16

Yvette had been beyond angry when she'd smelled the faint whiff of whiskey still clinging to Jacob. But as she sat stewing in her office, the anger fled and the sadness set in. If he'd been wallowing in whiskey, it was fair to assume that he'd been upset by his contact with Sienna. And if he'd been upset, that probably meant he still cared. And who could blame him? She still had her moments when she saw Isaac with his new someone, and that someone hadn't even been her best friend.

When she saw the devastated look in his eyes when she'd asked about Sienna, she'd resolved to cut him a break. A chapter in his life had ended, and he had every right to work through whatever emotions he was feeling.

Once they'd moved on to talking about the success of the store, the rain cloud hovering over his head had all but disappeared. They'd planned marketing strategies for the upcoming events, talked about ways to improve crowd control during the signings, and brainstormed front window display ideas.

When it was time to leave for the day, Yvette stopped in his office. "Woodlines?"

"Huh?" he asked as he looked up from his computer.

"Does Woodlines sound good? Or we could go to the brewery. I heard the new chef added a flourless cake to the menu. Noel said it's divine."

"Oh, right." He frowned. "I'm sorry, Yvette. I'm still not feeling one hundred percent. I think I better pass on dinner." Jacob closed his laptop and shoved it in a computer bag as he stood. "I'll be in tomorrow, and we can go over the café numbers to see how the first full week went."

"Okay, sure." She stepped out of his way as he brushed past her and headed for the front door. Following, she stopped at the checkout counter and watched as he slipped out the front door without looking back. A sharp stab of pain pierced her heart, and she clutched at her chest.

After the rocky morning, they'd had a good day and spent a good bit of time discussing future plans for the bookstore. She'd actually thought maybe her presence had helped him start to feel normal after the stressful weekend, but his brushoff told another story. She sighed and leaned against one of the bookshelves, wondering when she'd learn. He'd been interested for all of a week… and now? Who knew? But she wasn't setting herself up for another heartbreak. This was her sign she was in too deep, and it was time to face the inevitable. They were destined to be business partners and nothing more.

"Brinn, you can take off. I'll lock up tonight," she said.

Brinn glanced up, surprised, smoothing her long, sleek hair. "You're sure?"

Yvette eyed the young woman, feeling envious of her youth and the possibilities ahead of her. Brinn had recently graduated from college and had landed back in Keating Hollow, indicating to Yvette that she'd given the city a try and the one thing she knew for sure was that she wanted to come home... for good. Yvette didn't know why, but she could relate. She'd come home after college as well, only she'd brought Isaac with her, and they'd started a life together.

What would've happened if Yvette hadn't gotten married? Would she still be right here at her bookstore, pining over her business partner? She doubted it. Isaac had been the one to encourage her to open the store in the first place. For that, she had to thank him, because she couldn't imagine herself anywhere else. "Yes, I'm sure. Go out with your girlfriends, or get Rhys to take you out. You deserve a little fun in your life."

Brinn laughed. "Rhys? Seriously? We grew up together. My mom used to babysit him and has pictures of us in the bathtub together. I think I was two and he was four. I'm certain we can't recover from that humiliation."

Yvette laughed. "Okay, maybe not Rhys. But there are other cute boys in this town. Go find one and let me live vicariously."

"Yvette?" Brinn asked as she slipped out from behind the counter. "Are you all right?"

"Of course." Yvette forced a bright smile, even though she felt like she wanted to curl up in a ball and pretend the world didn't exist for a while. She needed to lick her wounds and come to terms with the fact that any fantasies she'd had about a relationship with Jacob were over. "I just want you to have some fun for a change. When's the last time you went out with Hanna?"

She shrugged. "Not since before the holidays. It's been busy."

"Well, how about you go find her and grab her for a night of dancing? Then tomorrow you can tell me all about the hot guy you met."

Brinn laughed. "You know what? I think I will." She

squeezed Yvette's hand and said, "And you know what you should do?"

"Watch *Practical Magic* for the twentieth time and gorge myself on Miss Maple's chocolates?"

"You should go to the brewery and ask Rhys out."

"Rhys? You've got to be kidding me. He's too young for me," Yvette said, shaking her head.

"No, he isn't." She rolled her eyes. "He's in his twenties. Come on, Yvette, you're not that old."

"Old enough," she muttered. Then she peered at Brinn. "Why Rhys?"

A mischievous smile claimed her lips. "Because Rhys is the best looking guy in town and if Jacob got wind of it… well a little jealousy can go a long way to helping a man get his head out of his backside."

Yvette stared at Brinn, her mouth hanging open. Then she threw her head back and laughed. When she finally caught her breath, she said, "You know, you just might be on to something there."

Brinn nodded. "We make a good team."

Yvette hadn't taken Brinn's suggestion of asking Rhys out seriously, but a half-hour later she still found herself sitting at the bar, eyeing the gorgeous man. He had his back to her, and she could see the muscles rippling across his shoulders. *He must work out,* she thought. There was no other explanation for that body. None of the other guys looked like that after the long days of moving beer cases around. It didn't hurt that he had dark hair, dark eyes, and a backside that made most woman salivate.

Unfortunately, Yvette wasn't most women. She'd also

known Rhys for most of his life and had never seen him as anything other than a friend. The idea of asking him out just to annoy Jacob was out of the question. She didn't want to play games with anyone. All she really wanted was a beer to drown her sorrows.

Rhys slid a dark stout over to her. "Dinner?"

"Yeah. I better go with—" A loud crash came from her father's office. Yvette was on her feet in seconds and right behind Rhys as he flung the door open to find Lincoln Townsend sprawled on the floor. A wooden chair had been knocked over, and one of the legs had split.

"Dad!" Yvette's chest ached with fear and emotion as she pushed Rhys out of the way and knelt by his side. His skin was gray and clammy and chilled to the touch. "Call an ambulance!"

Rhys picked up the office phone and dialed.

Yvette grabbed her dad's wrist and found a thready pulse. "He's alive," she said. "But his breathing is shallow and his skin... Good goddess," Yvette breathed. "He looks like we're losing him."

Rhys relayed the information to the 911 operator while she held her dad's hand, not having the slightest clue what to do to help him. Tears filled her eyes, and she whispered, "Don't you dare leave us now, old man. You still have to walk Noel down the aisle when Drew finally decides to make it official. And Faith, she's yet to meet her special someone. You have to be around to give whoever that is the third degree."

His eyes fluttered open and he blinked a few times before focusing on her. "What about you?" he whispered.

She smiled through the tears as relief rushed through her and made her head spin. "What about me?"

He cleared his throat. "I'm not going anywhere until you meet your someone."

Yvette laughed. "I'd certainly prefer it that way, and as long as I'm making requests, let's just say we expect another forty or fifty years, okay?"

"You don't ask for much, do you?" he said and tried to roll over, but he winced and clutched at his left arm.

"You're hurt," she said.

"It's just a bruise." He tried to push himself up into a sitting position using his right arm, but Rhys bent down and put a light hand on his chest.

"Just stay still, Lin," Rhys said gently. "The paramedics are on their way. Let them check you out before you make anything worse."

Her dad started to protest, but Yvette said, "Dad, please."

She didn't know if it was the fear in her voice or the effort it took to try to fight off Rhys, but Lin stopped struggling and rested his head back down on the wood floor. Rhys shrugged off his hoodie, balled it up, and placed it under the older man's head. "Don't worry, Lin. They'll be here any minute."

Yvette sat back on her heels, pulled her phone out of her pocket, and hit Noel's number.

"Keating Hollow Inn, this is Noel. How can I help you?"

"It's Yvette," she said into the phone. "There's been an accident. Dad fell—"

"Dad fell?" Noel shouted into the phone. "Where? When? Is he okay?"

"In his office, just a minute or so ago. The ambulance is on its way. Can you meet us at the emergency room and call Faith and Abby?"

"They don't need to—oomph." Lin rubbed at his chest.

Yvette's mind raced. Had he had a heart attack? Should she be shoving an aspirin in his mouth?

"They don't need to come to the emergency room," Lin finished.

Rhys chuckled. "Sure, Lin. You can't expect to pull this kind of drama and not have every Townsend sister lining up to tell you how to take care of yourself."

"Don't I know it," Lin grumbled.

"Yvette, are you still there?" Noel practically shouted into the phone.

"I'm here. Just keeping an eye on dad. What was that?"

"I said I'd call them, and I asked how he's doing. If he's complaining about the ambulance that's a good sign."

Her sister's words made Yvette let out a small, sad chuckle. "Yes, you're right. He's complaining. So he can't be that bad, right?"

"Right," Noel said. "I'll meet you in the emergency room as soon as I can."

"Drive safely. I'm going with dad in the ambulance." Just as she said the words, she heard the piercing sound of sirens drowning out everything else. "They're here. Gotta go."

Yvette scrambled out of the way as the paramedics rushed in. They checked Lin's vitals, gave him oxygen, and got him on the gurney in record time.

"Is he going to be all right?" Yvette asked as she ran alongside the gurney.

"We sure hope so," Vinn Cantor said. He was a sweet man who'd been on the job in Keating Hollow for over ten years. He'd been riding the same unit with Ferris Eros for over five years. Unless one of them was sick or on vacation when someone called for an ambulance, Vinn and Ferris were the two who showed up.

The two men lifted Lin into the vehicle. Vinn jumped in after him while Ferris held out his hand for Yvette. "Get in. We're almost ready to roll."

"Thanks," Yvette said and took a seat against the wall, while Vinn locked the gurney in place and checked Lin's vitals again.

Lin blinked up at the man, the oxygen mask still covering his face, making it difficult to talk.

Yvette reached out and took her dad's hand in hers. Then she leaned closer to him and said, "You always did have a flair for the drama."

Lin let out a small chuckle and squeezed Yvette's hand.

When Vinn was done, he glanced up and met Yvette's gaze. "I won't let anything happen to him."

She wanted to tell him he damned well better not let anything happen to her father, the man who was respected and loved by the entire town, but she held her tongue, knowing her words would only be spoken out of fear. Instead she said, "Thanks, Vinn. We all appreciate your help."

"Just doing my job," he said softly, but he nodded and tipped his hat.

"Sta lirting with my dier," Lin mumbled from beneath the oxygen mask.

Yvette frowned as she peered down at her father. "What?"

Lin flicked his gaze to Vinn and then to Yvette and back to Vinn again.

Vinn laughed. "He told me to stop flirting with his daughter."

"Dad," Yvette said, shaking her head in exasperation. "He's just being kind to me because… well, obviously this is kind of a scary situation." Though now that he was trying to protect her from the very single paramedic, she took that as a good sign that he'd be all right. In fact, as she watched her father, she noticed that his color was improving.

"I'll behave myself, Mr. Townsend. You have nothing to worry about," Vinn said, but he wasn't looking at Lin when he spoke. Instead, he was staring straight at Yvette. His smile widened, revealing a surprising dimple in his left cheek.

Something shifted in Yvette, and she started to see Vinn in

a different light. There was no denying he was a good looking man. His deep blue eyes, combined with that dimple, were enough to make any woman sit up and take notice. But combine his looks with his desire to care for the community, and he seemed downright irresistible.

Why hadn't Yvette ever considered him before? She knew the answer as soon as she contemplated the question. He was a good seven or eight years older than her, and she'd been married for the last decade. If Vinn asked her out, would she go? Last week she'd have said no. This week? Maybe.

Yvette shook her head. What was she doing thinking about dating the paramedic while her father was being rushed to the hospital? Was she that desperate for a date? *Pathetic,* she thought.

"What's wrong, Yvette?" Vinn asked her.

"Nothing. Just worried about my dad." She tightened her grip on Lin's hand and spent the remainder of the trip avoiding Vinn's gaze.

CHAPTER 17

Yvette grabbed Noel's hand when she spotted her father's oncologist heading for them. Since Lin was still under her care for the cancer, she'd been called in to check on him. Yvette and Noel stood at the same time. Faith hadn't arrived yet, and Abby was still out of town.

"Dr. Sims," Yvette said, as the doctor reached them. "How is he?"

"Is it the cancer?" Noel asked.

"Yes and no," Dr. Sims said, waving a hand to invite them to sit back down. When they were settled, she pulled up a chair so that she was sitting across from them. "This episode was caused by severe dehydration. It appears he just fainted. We have him hooked up to an IV, and we'll keep him overnight for observation, but I think he'll come out of this with just a few bumps and bruises."

"No broken bones?" Yvette asked. She'd been worried he'd fractured something when he went down.

"No broken bones," Dr. Sims confirmed. "We shot some x-rays, and everything is fine on that front. He's suffered some tissue damage, so he'll be sore for the better part of a week, I'd imagine, but he'll heal."

Yvette let out a sigh of relief, but Noel leaned forward, her hands fidgety. "Does this mean he needs to start treatments again?"

Dr. Sims frowned at Noel's question. "Start again?"

"Yes," Noel nodded. "You said this episode was and wasn't due to the cancer. Does that mean the last round didn't work as well as we hoped?"

Dr. Sims cleared her throat. "Were you under the impression he'd stopped treatments?"

"Yes," both Yvette and Noel said at the same time.

The two sisters looked at each other, and then Noel turned to the doctor and said, "He told us he was done with treatments for now. Is that not true?"

The doctor closed her eyes and muttered something unintelligible to herself. Then she shook her head and said, "Your father started a new round of chemo three weeks ago. It's likely the reason he passed out is because he had a treatment yesterday. I told him he shouldn't work for at least two or three days after any treatment. But from the looks of it, he was back at the brewery. Is that right?"

"Yes," Yvette said. "That's where he passed out."

"From now on, I'm only clearing him for six hours of work a week and at the brewery only. No work in the orchard. And he needs to be drinking water. No beer. No alcohol of any kind. Juice is fine but no soda. Want me to write this down?"

"Yes," Yvette said, knowing if she could show the doctor's words in writing to her stubborn father, she'd at least have a leg to stand on when he flat-out refused to do as she instructed.

The doctor made a note on the chart. When she looked up,

she said, "Listen, all three of us know Lin's going to do whatever it is he wants to do. But try to keep him from overdoing it and keep plenty of fluids in him. And while you're at it, feed him as many calorie-rich foods as you can find. I'd feel a lot better if he gained back those twenty pounds he's lost since the diagnosis."

"Dr. Sims," Noel asked, "can you tell us where we are with his cancer treatment? Is it worse? Should we be worried?"

Yvette held her breath while she waited for the doctor to answer. She didn't think she could take it if his condition had worsened.

"His numbers are looking better, but not enough for a break in treatments. I'm guessing he'll need at least another two or three rounds before we see the kind of numbers we're looking for. The answer to your question is that right now, he isn't getting worse. In fact, if he takes care of himself, I could easily say he's making progress. But if he exhausts himself again, infection could set in, and that could be catastrophic. I can't stress enough how important it is that he takes it easy over the next few months."

"If it's so important," Yvette said, "is it wise to let him work at the brewery? I know my father, and he really likes having his fingers in every aspect of the business. I'm not sure he can stick to six hours."

Dr. Sims grinned. "I was originally going to give him ten, but since we've discussed this before, I'm well aware of his tendency to overwork himself. That's why we're back at six. As far as not working at the brewery at all, I think it gives him a sense of purpose and community. And I'm certain those two things are worth it for his mental health. We just need to get him to start listening to his body."

"You're devious," Noel said, eyeing the doctor in admiration. "I like it."

Yvette laughed. "Dr. Sims isn't letting any patient of hers get out of line. That's for sure."

Dr. Sims chuckled and rose to her feet. "I do my best. If you're ready, you can go see your dad now. Tell him I said hi and that I outed him. Thanks to that release form he signed months ago, you two and your other sisters have full access to his medical condition. So don't hesitate to ask if you need me to explain what's going on."

Noel and Yvette rose as well. They both thanked the doctor for her candor and then headed for their dad's room.

They found him sitting propped up in the bed, sipping on something that looked an awful lot like hot chocolate.

"Who'd you charm that out of?" Noel asked him.

"The pretty brunette nurse who keeps coming in here and checking my IV bag," he said.

Yvette walked over and sat on the edge of his bed. His color was back, and he honestly looked better than he had in days. How had she been so blind that she hadn't seen how sick and exhausted he'd looked? "How are you feeling, dad?"

"Better now that I have this." He nodded to the hot chocolate. "The ride in the ambulance was something I could've done without, though."

"Yeah, about that—" Noel started.

Lin cut her off. "Your sister has a thing for one of the paramedics."

Noel blinked. "Faith has a thing for Vinn or Ferris?"

Lin chuckled while Yvette wondered if either would notice if she just slinked back out of the room.

"Not Faith," Lin said. "Yvette."

"Jacob is a paramedic?" Noel blurted out.

"Jacob?" Lin asked. "Jacob Burton?"

"Um..." Noel glanced at her sister and flushed as she mouthed, *sorry*.

"You're not getting involved with Jacob, are you?" Lin asked Yvette, concern coloring his tone. "Are you sure that's a good idea, Rusty?"

"No, dad, I'm not getting involved with him," she said, telling herself it wasn't a lie since she'd already decided they couldn't move forward with whatever relationship they'd started. "You're right, it would be a bad idea."

"Good, good," he said absently. "I don't want to see you hurt again."

She wasn't sure what he meant by that and decided it wasn't worth asking. She didn't want to be hurt any more than she already had.

"I was talking about Vinn," her father said. "He was flirting with her. They both deny it, but I know flirting when I see it."

Yvette gave Noel a he's-lost-his-mind look. "Dad was hallucinating due to his dehydration."

Noel raised both eyebrows and eyed her sister. "Vinn? Really?"

Yvette just shook her head. "No. He was just being nice to me because I was freaked out about dad passing out." She turned to her father. "We spoke with your doctor, Dad."

He stared up at the ceiling and sighed. "I figured you would."

Noel moved to the other side of her father's bed and sat opposite Yvette. "We know you're still getting treatments. Why did you make us believe you were done with them for now?"

He gritted his teeth, clearly uncomfortable being questioned by his two oldest daughters. "I just wanted some peace. That's all. Clair has been taking me to my appointments."

"Okay," Yvette said. "That's good, but don't you think we should be kept informed about your medical treatment?" She could hear the hurt in her own voice and she wanted to swallow her words. He didn't need a guilt trip while he was in the hospital. She just wanted him to take care of himself.

"I'm a grown man, Yvette," he said.

"I know that, Dad. But do you know how scared I was today when you went down at the brewery? I had no idea you'd had a treatment yesterday. If I had, maybe then I'd at least have understood what was going on. Instead, I was convinced you'd had a heart attack… or worse. I'm just asking that you keep us updated. If you don't want us going to your doctor visits or getting in your business, tell us to butt out. But at least let us know what's going on."

He glanced at both of his daughters. Yvette could see by his slightly irritated expression that he wanted to tell her to butt out right then and there, but because he was Lin Townsend and loved his daughters more than anything in the world, he nodded. "That's fair."

Noel smiled. "Thanks. There's one more thing."

He groaned. "What?"

"Your doctor said you're overworking yourself, and you've been restricted to six hours a week," Noel said.

Lin's eyes narrowed. "I was just dehydrated."

"So we've heard," Yvette said. "Dr. Sims says if you don't take care of yourself, you're at risk for infection. And let me tell you this right now, Dad, we're not letting that happen. So six hours at the brewery. That's it. And we're going to hold Clay and Rhys responsible."

"How about I just hand everything over and stay home in my recliner?" he asked in a clipped tone, his eyes flashing with anger. "You can hire me a nurse to wait on me hand and foot, and I'll just spend the rest of my life doing nothing but watching daytime television. Are those soaps your mother used to watch still on? Maybe I can finally find out what all the fuss was about."

"Nah, Dad, you don't have to watch soaps," Noel said. "You can binge watch just about anything on Netflix. You should give *The Walking Dead* a try. It's hugely popular."

"Why would I do that? I'm already living the life of the walking dead."

Yvette had to stifle a laugh. He was being so dramatic. "Noel's just messing with you, Dad. No one wants you to waste your days in the recliner."

"No?" He glared at Yvette. "Well, that's what will happen if I stop working at the brewery. Now that there isn't much to do with the orchard over the winter, I don't have anything else to do. Why do you think I offered to fill in for Clay?"

"You can still work six hours," Yvette said lamely, feeling awful for her father. She was finally able to see just how terrible and frustrating this illness was for her dad. It wasn't just the battling of the disease; it was everything else. Having his daughters take on the role of caretaker, being forced out of his business, and feeling like a spectator in his own life.

He snorted. "Great."

Yvette met Noel's gaze. Neither of them knew what to say. Yvette desperately wished she had a magic wand she could wave to make everything better for her father. And for maybe the first time in her adult life, she found herself feeling truly helpless.

CHAPTER 18

Yvette barely slept. After spending the evening with her dad in the hospital, she'd been exhausted, but every time she dozed off, she saw him lying unconscious on the floor of his office, his skin that sickly gray color. Only when she found him on the floor in her dreams, he didn't wake up.

She was up by five, unwilling to keep reliving the same dream over and over again. And even though her body ached from fatigue, she walked out of her house at five minutes to six and headed straight for Incantation Café.

Twenty minutes later, armed with the best coffee in town and two bear claws, she strode into the hospital and made a beeline for her dad's room. Technically, it wasn't visiting hours, but no one stopped her or said a word when she slipped past the nurse's station.

She found her dad propped up against the pillows, flipping through the morning news channels. "Good morning," she said, forcing the brightness in her tone.

He glanced over at her and a genuine smile tugged at his lips. "What are you doing here so early, Rusty?"

"Bringing my favorite father breakfast." She set the coffee and bag of pastries on the cart next to his bed. "I figured this would be better than anything they were serving."

He picked up the coffee cup and breathed in the rich aroma. "You are now officially my favorite daughter."

She rolled her eyes. "You're so easily bribed."

"That's probably true." He stuffed one of the bear claws in his mouth with the exuberance of a little kid.

She sipped her coffee and waited for him to polish off the pastry. Once he was done, she said, "You're in an awfully good mood this morning."

"Why wouldn't I be? They're springing me out of here any minute." He sucked down a swig of his coffee and let out a contented sigh. "You really know how to get back in my good graces, don't you?"

His statement startled a laugh out of her. "It would appear so," she agreed and sat down on the edge of his bed. "Listen, Dad, I'm pretty sure I owe you an apology."

He grabbed another bear claw, but before he bit into it, he gave her a confused glance. "For what?"

"For treating you like a little kid," she blurted. "For going behind your back to talk to your doctor without you. And most of all, for not listening all of these months when you've been telling us you need something more to do than just hanging around the house. We—I just don't want you to be sick anymore."

He reached out and grabbed her hand. "I don't want to be sick anymore either, love, but it's the hand I've been dealt, and I have to deal with it. It's my battle to conquer."

"Of course it is, but you don't have to do it alone. We're all here for you."

"I know," he said simply. "But you can't just set rules for me to abide by and hope the disease goes away. I've done my research. I'm fully aware that this is a type of cancer I could be living with for the rest of my life. And if I'm going to really live, then it's not going to be behind the television screen watching other people's pretend lives."

"I understand completely," she said with a nod. If anyone tried to get her to stay away from her business, that message would be dead on arrival. "And I think you should spend as many hours as you want at the brewery."

Lin eyed her with suspicion. "What happened? Judging by last night's conversation, I was certain this was a fight we were going to have over and over again. What changed?"

Yvette pointed to herself. "I did. First, I couldn't stop dreaming about you lying unconscious on the office floor. Then I realized that if someone tried to keep me away from my bookstore while I was in treatment, it might be the last thing they ever did. It's important for you to have something to live for other than us kids. I'm sorry we tried to take that away from you."

His wiry eyebrows shot up. "You did? How?"

"We sort of convinced your doctor that you don't really take it easy at work, and that's why she reduced your allotted time there."

"That's… all true," he said with a laugh. Then his eyes glittered as he asked, "You know what, Yvette?"

"What's that, dad?"

"I wasn't going to listen anyway, so it's really no big deal. I'll work when I want to, and I'll be much more careful about taking care of myself, but that's all I can promise."

"That's all I need," Yvette said, leaning down to give him a hug. His warm arms wrapped around her, giving her one of his legendary hugs.

"Thank you, my sweet girl," he whispered in her ear.

"For what?" she asked.

"For loving your old man enough that you showed up here before the crack of dawn with goods from the Pelshes' cafe." He grinned. "What do you say? Should we make a second stop there when you give me a lift home?"

"Definitely. More caffeine and sugar are always the correct answers."

"That's what I thought," he said with a nod.

"Good morning, Ms. Townsend," the night nurse said as she swept into the room holding a clipboard. She turned to Lin. "Ready to blow this popsicle stand?"

"You have no idea just how much," he said.

"Excellent." She handed him a file of paperwork. "Inside you'll find instructions from Dr. Sims for your continued recovery. Don't forget to hydrate."

"Yes, Ma'am," he said. "I certainly will. And if I don't, I'm sure my daughters are on standby, figuring out who will be my caretaker."

"There's no need to wonder, Dad," Yvette said. "I have a feeling I've already been nominated for that prestigious honor."

"Heaven help us," he said, and as the nurse bustled back out of the room again, Lin patted the bed for his daughter to join him again. "Take a seat."

She did as she was told and waited.

It took him a moment to form the words, but when he did, he got straight to the point. "I know you're seeing Jacob Burton."

"How did you… who told you this?"

Her father brushed a lock of her hair behind her ear. "No one, love. Though he did come here last night looking for you. That was my first clue."

"Wait, what? Jacob was here?" she asked.

"In the flesh."

She was stunned. After the brush-off earlier in the day, she'd gotten the impression he wouldn't be calling her again.

"You lied to me about him. Why, Yvette?"

She glanced over at her tough-as-nails father and shrugged. "I guess because I didn't want you to be disappointed in me."

Her father sucked in a sharp breath. "Why would you think that? You're entitled to a date every now and then."

"Yes, but experiments in mixing business with pleasure have always ended poorly for me. You'd think I'd learn, but…"

"No one ever does when it comes to matters of the heart," he said, patting her hand. "Forget anything I said about your choice to date Jacob Burton. He's a good man from what I can tell, and he'd be so lucky if you decided he was worth your time."

"He is a good man," Yvette said sadly. "I just don't think he's interested in being *my* good man."

Lin chuckled softly. "That's not what I saw when he came barging in here last night looking for you. I suppose there's a chance I could be wrong…" he shrugged, "I'm not though."

The nurse charged back in with a wheelchair before Yvette could say another word. "Ready for the express train out of here?"

"You know it," Lin said and took his place in the wheelchair. "My daughter's got it from here." He turned to Yvette. "Let's go. There's another bear claw or two just waiting for me."

CHAPTER 19

Thursday morning dawned bright and sunny, a rarity for Keating Hollow in January. Jacob stood on his deck bundled in a scarf and jacket and felt a longing he hadn't experienced in many years. Maybe not since he'd been a freshman in high school and had fallen hard for Mary Jean Hopkins, the transfer student from Austin, Texas who'd moved back home after her parents separated.

He couldn't stop wishing Yvette was standing next to him, enjoying the incredible view of the redwoods. He could almost feel her nestled beside him, smiling and chattering on about something a customer had said. The past two days had been torture working with her. She'd been her polite, cheery self, but also distant as if she'd already accepted that whatever had been going on with them was over.

Jacob hated it. He wanted to march into her office and tell her everything, to explain that he'd just learned about his daughter and that if his life hadn't suddenly taken a left turn, he'd be sweeping her off her feet and praying that she fell in love with him. He wouldn't though. What purpose would that serve other than making him feel better? Laying his crap on her would only make things worse.

His phone buzzed, interrupting his thoughts. He glanced down and saw it was from Yvette. The contractor had arrived to talk about putting a window in his office, and she needed his input. Jacob closed his eyes and muttered a curse. He'd forgotten all about the window. It was completely unnecessary now that he'd decided he needed to leave Keating Hollow, only he hadn't had the courage to tell Yvette yet. He'd been waiting to talk to Sienna this weekend and find out more about her future plans.

I'll be there in ten minutes, he typed back.

The green light lit up indicating she was typing something back, but then it disappeared. He waited, expecting a reply, but none came. Jacob shoved the phone into his pocket, pulled out his keys, and headed for his truck. It was time to face the music.

"YVETTE?" Jacob called as he knocked on her office door. When there was no reply, he cracked the door open and peeked in. The room was empty. He'd already checked his office, but there hadn't been any sign of Yvette or the contractor.

"She's not here," Brinn said from behind him.

Jacob spun and eyed the young woman who'd been busy helping a customer when he'd walked into the store. "She just texted me fifteen minutes ago."

Brinn nodded. "She got a call from her niece's school and rushed out of here in a panic. Apparently they couldn't get in touch with Noel, so they called Yvette."

He felt himself go cold inside as he remembered the vibrant

young girl he'd met at Lincoln Townsend's the night he'd had dinner with them. "Daisy's hurt?"

"I think so, but I didn't get any of the details."

"Thanks, Brinn."

He pulled out his phone and sent Yvette a text, asking if everything was all right. He hadn't expected a return text so soon, but she immediately typed back, *No. Can you come to the school? Daisy and I need a ride.*

I'm on my way.

Without another thought, he rushed out of the store and jumped into his truck. The school was only two blocks away, and when he pulled up to the curb where Yvette and Daisy were waiting, he quickly learned why she'd needed him to come get them. Her bike was leaning against the wall of the building, and Daisy was holding a blood-soaked towel over her left eye, whimpering as Yvette tried to soothe her.

Jacob ran around the truck and helped them both in. Once he was back behind the wheel, he glanced at Yvette. "The emergency room or the healer's office?"

"The healer's office. I already called Gerry, and she's confident she'll be able to stitch her up and tend to her bruises," Yvette said. She had her arm wrapped around her niece and was gently stroking her.

"You got it." He put the truck in gear and headed for the center of town.

"Thank you for coming for us," she said. "I didn't drive to work today, so I only had my bike, and Noel is out in Eureka running errands today."

"You're welcome," Jacob said. "I'm happy to help."

"Auntie?" Daisy said with a whimper.

"Yes, sweet pea?" Yvette said, her voice tender.

"My head hurts a lot."

"I bet it does," Yvette soothed. "We don't have too much

further to go, and then Gerry will fix you right up, make you good as new. Can you hang in there for me?"

"Okay." The little girl's voice was so meek and pathetic that Jacob longed to scoop her up in his arms and shield her from everyone and everything.

"What happened?" he asked.

"I fell," Daisy said, her bottom lip trembling.

Yvette's eyes turned dark and stormy as she added, "She had help with that fall."

Anger balled in this pit of his stomach and Jacob had to work to keep his expression neutral. "I hope he—"

"She," Yvette corrected.

"Sorry," he said. "I hope *she* apologized."

"Not yet," Yvette said with a sigh. "But her parents have been called, and I'm sure the school will deal with it appropriately. If not, they are going to have one very upset Townsend clan storming the gates."

Not just the Townsends, he thought. Even though he knew it was irrational, he couldn't help but feel protective after seeing the injured child so upset. If Yvette or her sister needed him for anything, he'd be there. But then he remembered that he was planning to leave town sooner rather than later.

He frowned and shook his head. What was he thinking? He wasn't a part of their family. None of them would learn to count on him in a crisis. The only reason he was taking them to the healer at the moment was because he'd texted at just the right time. Sadness washed over him, and he wasn't sure why. All he knew was in the moment, he liked that he felt needed.

Healer Gerry was waiting for them when they got to the clinic. She took Daisy and Yvette back into one of the patient rooms without even having them fill out any paperwork. Jacob took a seat and waited.

Forty-five minutes later, Yvette and Daisy reappeared. The

little girl had stitches over her left eye and an angry discoloration that looked like it was going to be one heck of an impressive bruise.

"Jacob?" Yvette said. "You didn't have to wait for us."

He stood and set the magazine he'd been skimming aside. "Sure I did. I wasn't going to let you two walk home."

She gave him a grateful smile and took Daisy's hand in hers. "Okay, thanks. We're ready. We just need to stop and get a potion from Charming Herbals to help Daisy control the headache. Is that okay?"

"Of course."

After Yvette settled the bill with the healer, Jacob chauffeured them around and then took them back to the inn. Noel met them outside and wrapped her arms around Daisy, fussing and cooing and apologizing for not being there.

"Aunt Vette and Uncle Jacob took good care of me," Daisy said, putting on her brave face.

Jacob met Yvette's amused gaze. She shrugged as if to say, *what can you do?*

"They did, huh?" Noel tucked a lock of Daisy's hair behind one ear. "That's good. They must love you a lot."

Daisy nodded and said, "Can I go inside now? My head still hurts."

"Of course, baby," Noel said and gave her a kiss on the top of her head. "Go on and get into bed. I'll be right in."

Daisy disappeared through the backdoor of the inn's residence. As soon as the door closed, Noel wrapped her arms around Yvette. "Thank you so much for taking care of her. If she'd had to wait for me—"

"But she didn't," Yvette said. "And she's going to be fine. Gerry said to follow up with her about watching for a concussion and how to care for the stitches."

"Oh, goddess. A concussion?" Noel asked.

"Gerry said she doesn't think Daisy has one, but she wants you to watch for symptoms just in case." Yvette handed her the bag she was still holding. "This is the headache potion. Gerry said for her to take it with a bit of food as needed."

"Okay." Noel nodded and wiped a lone tear from her cheek. "Sorry, I was just so worried when the school called and said she hit her head. It killed me to not be there."

"I know," Yvette said. "Call me later and let me know how she's doing, okay?"

"I will." Noel turned to Jacob. "Thank you for all your help. That was very kind of you."

"You're welcome," he said, trying not to feel like he'd intruded on a family moment.

Noel took a step closer and flung her arms around him, too. She hugged him tightly and said, "You're good people, Jacob Burton. I think we're lucky to have you here in Keating Hollow."

He pulled back and gave her an awkward smile, not at all sure what to say.

"Daisy's waiting for you," Yvette said. "Go in and we'll get out of your hair."

"Right." She waved and then hustled back into her house.

Jacob and Yvette were just getting in the truck when an SUV with the words *Keating Hollow Sheriff's Department* scrawled across the doors pulled in right beside them. Drew jumped out and ran into the house. Jacob heard him call, "Daisy!" just before the door slammed shut.

"He's really fallen for that little girl, hasn't he?" Jacob asked Yvette.

"No doubt. She's an easy child to love," Yvette said. "She's head over heels for him, too. My heart nearly explodes when I see the three of them together. Noel had such a hard time after her first husband left. It took her a while to let Drew in, but thank goodness she did. They're perfect for each other."

"They look like it," Jacob said, recalling seeing them together at Clay and Abby's wedding. The obvious love between them had been almost nauseating to the man who'd sworn off women. But now when he saw them together, he found himself longing for that kind of passion. It wasn't something he'd ever had with Sienna. And now he was starting to wonder why he'd ever thought they were right for each other.

"I'm starving. Do you want to have some lunch?" Yvette asked him.

Her question startled him, but he recovered quickly and said, "Sure. Lunch would be great. Where do you want to go? Woodlines?"

She shook her head and pointed to her shirt. There were bloodstains from where Daisy had clutched her. "I need to change before we go back to the store. I figured we'd get lunch there. I have some leftover pasta I can heat up."

"You got it." Nervous energy filled Jacob as he pulled into her driveway five minutes later. The last time he'd been alone with her inside of her house, they'd spent the night together. He'd barely known her then and hadn't been able to keep his hands off her. What was going to happen now that he was pretty sure he was half in love with her?

Yvette led the way into her home. The living room was decorated with a white couch and matching armchairs. Turquoise washed wood furniture brightened the room and made it look like something you'd see in a beach town. Funny, he hadn't noticed the last time.

She waved for him to sit at the bar in the kitchen and went to work on reheating their lunch.

But instead of sitting, he rummaged through her fridge and

found a bottle of white wine. Without asking, he poured her a glass and handed it to her. "You look like you could use a drink."

She took the glass and let out a small laugh. "Do I look that bad?"

"No," he said, giving her a small smile. "You look beautiful. It's your eyes that are giving you away. What's wrong, Yvette?"

Tears instantly filled her pretty brown eyes and she shook her head.

Oh damn, he thought and instinctively moved to wrap his arms around her. "What is it, Yvette? Whatever it is, I'm here."

"I just… I don't know." The tears spilled down her cheeks and she pulled away from him, wiping angrily at her face. "It's stupid."

"I doubt that," he said, wishing he could do something, anything, to take her pain away. "Were you scared for Daisy?"

"Of course, but that's not…" She shrugged one shoulder. "Maybe it is why I'm upset. My adrenaline was running pretty high there for a while, and now my emotions are all over the place."

"She's okay, you know," he said, wanting to pull her back into his arms, but he gave her the space she obviously needed and leaned against the counter.

"Yeah, I know. I just…" She closed her eyes. "I love that little girl so much." Her eyes opened, and she met his gaze unflinchingly when she said, "I told Isaac almost a year ago that I was ready to start a family."

"What did he say?" Jacob could see the longing all over her face now, and it wasn't hard to figure out that taking care of her niece had brought her own broken dreams into focus.

She snorted. "That he wasn't ready. He wanted to wait a year or two to have more time for just us before we started having kids. I guess the truth was he wanted more time with *Jake* before he was bogged down with baby duty."

"Or he knew he was living a lie and didn't have the courage to face it yet," Jacob said.

Her face crumpled, and the tears came harder. "Don't defend him, Jacob."

He couldn't help it. He couldn't stand there doing nothing while she was in such pain. "I'm not defending him. Not at all. Come here," he said, holding his arms open again.

Without hesitation, she walked into his embrace and rested her head on his shoulder. "I'm sorry."

"For what?" He stroked her back.

"For breaking down on you like this." She sniffed. "I know this must be a nightmare situation, being forced to listen to me complain about how I'd hoped to be a mother by now."

"It's not a nightmare," he said, truly meaning it. The realization surprised him, but he *wanted* to be there. Wanted to be the one she leaned on. He thought of Sienna and the baby girl he hadn't yet met. Would he have been so willing to start a family if she'd asked?

Yes.

The answer was instantaneous. He'd always wanted kids, wanted a family of his own. He couldn't imagine telling her no. But then he'd never told her no to anything else either. "I get it, Yvette. I had dreams too, before Sienna left."

"You want kids?" she asked, her eyes dry now.

"Always have." He stared down at her, everything inside of him aching to kiss her. There was no denying the attraction between them. That had been instantaneous. But there was also something else, a connection that made them understand each other, a connection he'd never felt before and knew was extremely rare. He couldn't let that go, could he? If they were so perfect for each other, they'd find a way to make their circumstances work somehow, right? Before he could stop himself, he tilted his head down and brushed his lips over hers.

She hesitated as if she wasn't sure she should be kissing him, but then her fingers curled into his shirt and she opened to him.

He tightened his hold on her and gave himself over to the emotion consuming him. They stood locked together, kissing, tasting, teasing for a long time, until finally, Yvette pulled back and smiled up at him.

"Well, that was certainly unexpected," she said.

"I like surprises," he said, lightly trailing his fingertips over her cheek. "Was it okay I did that?"

She chuckled softly. "I think I'd be lying if I said no."

"Good." He bent his head again and stole another kiss, not wanting the moment to end.

She melted into him, sinking into the kiss with a sigh, but just when he was ready to take things further, she placed her hand against his chest and pressed lightly. "I think lunch is ready."

"I'm not hungry," he said, staring at her lips.

She laughed. "Maybe not, but I am." Yvette stepped back and pulled a casserole dish from the oven. The scent of garlic filled the air and his stomach rumbled. She glanced over her shoulder. "What was that you were saying about not being hungry?"

"I wasn't when I had you in my arms. But now that you've left me high and dry, it appears I could eat."

Yvette rolled her eyes and placed two plates of pasta on the kitchen bar. "We're gonna need a refill on the wine."

He obliged and after she was seated, he joined her. As they dug into the fettuccini alfredo, peace settled over Jacob, and he decided that if he could do this with her for the rest of his life, he was certain he'd die a contented and happy man.

CHAPTER 20

Yvette floated into work on Friday morning. After lunch the day before, despite the garlic, she and Jacob had engaged in an epic make-out session. And while they'd been together before, she hadn't been ready to invite him into her bed just yet. This time was different. She had a whole lot of emotions swirling around, and she wanted to be sure they weren't just caught up in the moment.

When she'd told Jacob she wanted to wait, she'd expected him to protest, but to her surprise, he'd wholeheartedly agreed and kissed her one last time before reluctantly saying goodbye. Then he'd surprised her by picking up her bike from the school and delivering it to her garage. She hadn't even known he'd done it until he'd texted later to let her know where to find it.

Her heart had melted right on the spot.

"Good morning, gorgeous," Jacob said.

She turned and found him at the café bar, making a latte. "Do you think you can make one of those for me?"

"I'm already on it." He poured the steamed milk into two

different cups and then handed her one. After doctoring his with a bit of sugar, he secured the top and moved out from behind the counter to stand next to her. "Do you have plans for lunch today?"

"Not that I know of. Why, what did you have in mind?" Her mind immediately flashed back to the day before, and heat crawled up her neck.

"Are you blushing?" he asked, eyeing her. "Yes, I think you are. Are you having impure thoughts, Ms. Townsend?"

"I was, um, just thinking about yesterday's lunch and wondering if that's what you were getting at."

He chuckled then frowned. "Unfortunately, no. There's something I need to talk to you about. I was hoping we could go somewhere less… tempting."

"I see. Now I'm intrigued," she said, dying to know what it was he wanted to say. Did he want to take their relationship to the next level now that he'd had time to get over his meeting with Sienna? Her heart skipped a beat just thinking about it. Even though she'd told herself numerous times to not get involved with him, she knew that she was kidding herself. She could no more resist him than she could a piece of flourless chocolate cake.

He ignored her comment and said, "Woodlines at one?"

"Sure. As long as Brinn is here, it shouldn't be a problem."

"I'll be here," Brinn called from the checkout counter. "I'll take my lunch early."

"It's a date then," Jacob said and raised his latte in a mock toast. "Until then, you can find me in my office unpacking the latest shipment."

Yvette watched him leave. His shoulders were hunched over, and she could've sworn she heard him muttering something to himself. Something was wrong. She could feel it. And it was then she knew that whatever he wanted to talk about at lunch was something she didn't want to hear.

~

AT A QUARTER TO ONE, Yvette dragged herself out of her office and met Jacob at the front of the store.

"Ready?" he asked.

She nodded and followed him out onto the sidewalk. A foreboding had settled over her, and with each step, she had to fight to keep from turning around and running back into the bookstore. But then he placed his hand on the small of her back, and she started to relax. The familiarity calmed her.

Yvette smiled up at him. "Did you finish checking in the new inventory?"

"Yep. Everything is arranged by author and genre."

"Good. I'll start stocking when we get back," she said.

"Oh, I should've told you sooner, but I'm going to have to take off after lunch. I have a friend coming into town for the weekend that I have to meet." His tone was wooden, and he sounded strange.

"Jacob? Are you all right?" she asked.

He glanced down at her. "Sure. Why?"

She shrugged one shoulder. "I don't know. You just didn't sound like yourself."

Jacob didn't respond, and her stomach clenched, that worry settling over her again. She told herself she'd wait until after lunch to ask him anymore questions. It was certainly possible he was just nervous about whatever it was he needed to say.

The restaurant wasn't all that busy, and they were seated right away.

"Wine?" Jacob asked.

"Sure." She really wasn't in the mood for wine, but she

wanted to be prepared in case the talk went as badly as she feared.

The waiter took their orders. Yvette went with a salmon salad, and Jacob chose the crab cakes. Neither of them said a word until after the waiter brought their wine.

"Thank you," Jacob said to Wyatt and then picked up his glass and downed nearly half of it.

Yvette couldn't take it anymore and leaned forward, her elbows on the table. "Whatever it is you have to say, I think you better just tell me."

"You're right. I—" His gaze suddenly locked on something over her shoulder as his mouth dropped open and his eyes went wide.

"What is it, Jacob?" she asked, glancing behind her. All she saw was a woman with long dark hair wearing a black dress that showed off every one of her perfect curves. And in her arms was a sweet baby girl with a mass of curly dark hair. She was dressed in a red wool jacket, black pants, and the most adorable little Mary Jane shoes. "Holy cow, that baby is cute."

Yvette turned her attention back to Jacob only to find he was out of his chair, his eyes still locked on the woman. "Jacob, what's going on?"

He glanced down at her, his mouth working but no sound coming out.

"There you are!" the woman said and strode over to Jacob. "I thought we'd never find you."

Jacob stared awestruck at the child.

"Do you want to hold her?" the woman asked him, her lips curving into an adoring smile as she turned her attention to the child.

"Yes," Jacob breathed.

The woman stroked the child's hair and whispered, "Okay, Skye, it's time to go to Daddy."

Daddy? Had this woman just indicated that Jacob was the child's father?

Jacob, who appeared to have forgotten that Yvette was even still in the restaurant, held out his hands and took the little girl in his arms. She snuggled against his chest and closed her eyes.

"We tried to find your place, but I couldn't remember the road," the woman was saying to him. "So I checked out that little bookstore... real *quaint,* Jacob. I can see why your father thinks you'll be back at Bayside Books within the year. Not much of a challenge, huh?"

Yvette, fuming at the woman's dismissal of her store, stood and stretched out her hand. "Hello, I'm Yvette Townsend, Jacob's business partner."

"Hello. I guess you figured out who I am," the woman said as she nodded to her child. "It was a long trip from L.A., but I promised Jacob we'd come up so we could spend the weekend together. He and Skye have a lot of catching up to do."

"Sienna," Jacob said, finally finding his voice. "Do you mind giving us just a minute?" He still had the child in his arms and was stroking her back as she rested her head on his shoulder.

"Well, I don't—" Sienna started.

"No, no," Yvette forced out, her insides churning with raw emotions. A lot had occurred to her in the past few moments. Sienna, his ex-fiancée, and *their* daughter were spending the weekend with him. Is that what he'd wanted to tell her over lunch? Why hadn't he told her about Skye before now? Had he just been playing her the entire time? He'd told her all about his breakup with Sienna, but he'd conveniently left out anything about the little girl locked in his arms. She wanted to ask why. Wanted to demand to know how he could spend the day before kissing her while knowing all along that his ex was coming to spend the weekend. "I should go. You two... um, enjoy lunch. I've got a meeting I have to get to."

"Yvette!" Jacob called after her.

She paused at the front door of the restaurant and glanced back at him. He hadn't moved, but his eyes were full of guilt and were silently pleading for her to understand. She shook her head once and then rushed out of the restaurant. Her chest was tight, and she was having trouble breathing. It took her a moment to realize it was because a sob had gotten caught in her throat and frustrated tears had started to roll down her cheeks.

"Dammit." She forced out the sob she'd been holding back and tried to suck in air. She couldn't go back to the bookstore like this. And she wasn't even sure she could go home. The thought of being in her house where she'd been with Jacob the day before was too much at the moment. She needed to be somewhere she wouldn't have to see or even think about Jacob.

Yvette pulled out her phone and hit Abby's number.

Her sister picked up on the first ring. "Hey, you," she said when she answered. "Did you miss me?"

"Are you up for a golf cart ride?" Yvette asked.

Her sister hesitated for a moment then asked, "Are you okay?"

"No. Not even close."

"Got it," Abby said. "I can be ready in ten minutes."

"I'll be there." Yvette ended the call and headed for her Mustang parked in front of the store.

CHAPTER 21

Jacob stared after Yvette and knew he'd just completely messed up. He'd been intending to tell her about Skye at lunch, but it was clear he shouldn't have waited. The smart thing would've been to tell her right after he'd gotten back from Los Angeles, to explain why he was so distant and had decided they shouldn't date. But he'd been far too messed up to think rationally.

"Looks like Yvette is a lot more than just your business partner," Sienna said, not bothering to hide the derision in her tone. Her lips were twisted into the crooked scowl she wore when she was angry.

"Does it matter?" he asked her, wondering how she could possibly care.

"It does if she's going to spend time around *my* daughter."

If it hadn't been for the precious little girl in his arms, he would've stalked right out of the restaurant and never looked back. "Sienna, cut the crap. Yvette and I are friends." That was the truth. Sienna didn't need to know that he was falling for her, especially because he was certain he'd just messed up whatever it was they'd gotten back the day before. "And even if we were a couple, you should count your blessings Yvette might be in Skye's life. She's a wonderful, loving aunt. You don't have anything to worry about there."

"I'll be the judge of that." She sat down in Yvette's empty seat and took a big swig of the untouched wine. "What's for lunch?"

He sighed and sat across from her, still cradling Skye in his arms. She smelled of baby powder and a sweetness he couldn't put his finger on. "Crab cakes and salmon salad. Or you can just order something else."

"Crab cakes will do," she said and placed the linen across her lap.

"Fine," he said as Skye wiggled in his arms. He pulled her away from his chest and stared at the smiling, squirmy baby. She was gorgeous with her huge amber eyes and sweet-as-pie dimples. "You're a pretty little thing, aren't you, Skye?" he said softly.

"You're not telling her anything she doesn't already know," Sienna said and tipped the wine glass to her lips again.

He raised one eyebrow. "Careful, Si. You sound a little jealous."

"Please." She rolled her eyes. "I'm just tired of all the conversation revolving around the baby."

Jacob frowned. He'd been wrong. Sienna didn't sound jealous. She sounded resentful, and he started to wonder what Skye's daily life was like. He bounced the baby on his knee and said, "Why don't you tell me what you've been up to this last year? Are you still working ten- to twelve-hour days at Enchanted Bliss?"

"At least twelve," she said, leaning forward now. "We're turning the Aspen property into the flagship store, so it requires my constant attention. I want to get every detail right."

"I'm sure it will be perfect," Jacob said. When they'd been opening the L.A. store, everything she did for the business was well thought out and well received. As long as she didn't flake out and leave the daily operations to a teenager again, the store would likely thrive.

"Thanks for that." Her shoulders relaxed, and she sat back in the chair, draining Yvette's wine glass. She raised the glass in the air and signaled the waiter for a refill. "And thanks for not immediately asking 'what about Skye.' I swear to the gods that if I get that question one more time I'm going to scream my lungs out. It's as if no one can fathom how a woman can possibly shove a baby out of her vag *and* have a career."

Jacob stared at her, wondering if she'd always been so crass. No, he didn't think so. In fact, she sounded a lot like Brian. His friend had always said inappropriate things, only he'd done it for the laughs. Sienna wasn't trying to entertain anyone; She was venting. "Um, I hate to be that guy, but in the interest of knowing how my daughter is being raised, where is she while you're working?"

Her eyes flashed with anger. "I make sure my daughter is taken care of, Jacob."

"Obviously," he said, not buying into whatever fight she was trying to start. He held the baby up as if showing her off. "Look at her. She's perfect. I'm just wondering who she spends her days with."

She sighed heavily. "If you must know, my mother has been taking her. Is that acceptable?"

"Of course it is," he said, more than a little annoyed at her hostility. "You don't have to get defensive. I'm just asking questions so I can understand how my daughter is being raised. Don't you think that's reasonable?"

She shrugged. "I guess."

The food arrived, and Sienna dug into the crab cakes with abandon. Jacob ignored the salad in front of him and spent the entire lunch making faces at Skye and feeling his heart nearly split in two from all the love filling him up. He knew the moment he'd laid eyes on her that he'd change his entire life just to be near her, to watch her grow up and be a part of her life.

"I assume this means you'll be raising Skye in Aspen then?" Jacob asked her.

She shoved in the last bite of crab cake and gave a noncommittal shrug.

"You're not honestly thinking of leaving the flagship store under someone else's management, are you?" he asked, already knowing the answer.

"Of course not." She pushed the plate away and started nibbling on his untouched salmon.

"So why wouldn't Skye grow up there?" he asked, suddenly concerned Sienna was going to pawn their daughter off on her mother, who had a small two-bedroom apartment in Long Beach.

"Jacob, can we talk about this back at the house? I'm trying to enjoy my wine."

He stared at the selfish creature sitting across from him and just felt sad. She seemed very unhappy with her life. She'd been much happier when they'd been together, he noted.

"Stop staring at me like that," Sienna said. "You're making me nervous."

"I'm just trying to understand what's going on with you, that's all," Jacob said.

"What's going on is that I was just cleared to drink, and since we're here in a restaurant with a bar, I'm having one or three. You should learn to lighten up." She flashed him a fake smile. "You should have a couple too. Then it won't hurt as much when she starts screaming at the top of her lungs."

"You wouldn't do that, would you, little lady?" Jacob asked his daughter.

"Just give her five minutes," Sienna said. "Then you'll be running out of here as fast as humanly possible."

Sienna's mood didn't improve as the afternoon wore on. After her lunchtime wine binge, Jacob had insisted on driving her car as he took them both back to his place. She hadn't been crazy about the idea, but when he'd said there was no way he was letting her behind the wheel with his daughter, guilt flashed over her features and she agreed.

"I can't believe you live here," she said as they were winding their way up the mountain.

"Why not?" He'd always preferred dramatic views. In his mind, his choice of home wasn't much different than the beach house they'd shared. The houses were a similar style, but instead of a view of the ocean, he had one of the gorgeous redwoods.

"It's just so… isolated. And the town—" She shook her head. "I know you said you loved it here as a kid, but honestly, Jacob, it's just so… I don't know, basic."

She meant there wasn't an entire street of designer shops and multiple Michelin-starred restaurants. He wanted to scold her for being a snob, but he held his tongue, not wanting to fight. "I like basic."

"I guess that's why we were never really all that compatible," she said with a shrug.

He gave her a disgusted side-eye glance. They weren't compatible because she'd apparently been in love with his best friend for years. "You know I was willing to live wherever you wanted."

"That's true," she said, nodding. "But it's hard to enjoy something when your partner is apathetic all the time."

He hadn't been apathetic, had he? Hadn't he taken her on every vacation she asked for? Made the reservations at all her favorite restaurants? Helped her open the spa she'd always wanted? Sure, he hadn't always been excited about her trips that seemed to be more centered around socializing with the rich and beautiful people of southern California than on actually exploring and enjoying new places, but he'd gone.

"Stop looking at me like that," she snapped. "You and I both know you hated my friends and the parties I made you go to. You might have been there physically, but you were almost never there mentally. All you wanted to do was hike or surf or some other outdoor thing." She visibly shuddered. "I've always been more of an indoor girl."

He couldn't argue with her on that one. She'd never pretended to be anything other than who she was. But then neither had he. "I guess the same could be said for you, Sienna. You only tried surfing once, and I never did get you out on a hiking trail."

"Like I've always said, I don't do the sun unless it's by the pool."

"Right." Jacob glanced back at the little girl sleeping in her car seat. Her sweet face made his heart burst all over again. And while he really wanted nothing to do with Sienna ever again, he'd endure her drama until the end of time if it meant he could have a place in his daughter's life.

"Now we're talkin'," Sienna said as the house came into view. "You always did have great taste in real estate."

"Thanks." He parked her Lexus in his garage and then fumbled around until he freed Skye from the car seat. He eventually emerged from the garage with Skye and the diaper bag to find Sienna on the phone, arguing with someone.

"Yes, I'm with Jacob. That was the entire point of coming here," she said into the phone.

Jacob started to make his way up the steps, wanting to get the baby out of the cold, but he froze when he heard her next words.

"Come on, Bri, give me a break. I'm doing what you asked. What more do you want from me?"

What he asked? Was Brian the reason why she'd told Jacob about his child? Had she only come clean because Brian had forced her hand? Jacob hadn't spoken to his ex-friend since Sienna had run off to be with him. But Jacob had to admit that if Brian knew Skye was Jacob's child, he'd insist Sienna tell him about it. He hated lies. It had been part of the reason the betrayal had been so brutal. He'd never have expected his friend to behave toward him in such a way.

"No, I haven't. I just got here. Fine. I'll call you tonight." She ended the call. When she turned around, she jumped as if she hadn't expected to see him there. "Were you eavesdropping?"

"Not on purpose." At least it hadn't started out that way.

"Well, I guess you figured out that was Brian," she said as she swept up the stairs past him.

"Yes. I got that impression." He handed her the key to unlock the door while he continued to cradle Skye.

She got the door open and strode in, letting out a small gasp when she spotted his view. He followed her and set the diaper bag down on his coffee table.

"It's lovely, Jacob," she said softly, sounding for the first time that day like the woman he'd once known and loved. "I can see why you love it. Still a little remote for my taste, but it's much better than what I was imagining."

He refrained from rolling his eyes. Her snobbery knew no

bounds. "It'll do." He reluctantly lifted the baby off his shoulder and started to hand her to Sienna, but she took a step back and shook her head.

"This is your weekend, Jacob. That means you're the primary caregiver."

He frowned at her. "So you're not even going to hold her while I unload your car?"

"Nope. I'll take care of the car. You just do your dad thing." She swept back outside and strolled down the front steps, leaving Jacob with his mouth hanging open. He couldn't quite figure out what was going on. Sienna, as far as he knew, had never voluntarily carried a suitcase in her life. She was a big fan of being pampered and was willing to pay for it.

Being pampered was the basis for Enchanted Bliss and why that business was so successful. Sienna had taken every expectation she'd ever had of being catered to and had folded them into the business to create the ultimate luxury experience. For her to grab her own bags when someone else was willing to do it was just bizarre.

But as Jacob sat in his recliner making faces at Skye and bouncing her on his knee, Sienna hauled in bag after bag and a mountain of baby supplies without complaint. When she was done, she headed straight for his kitchen and poured herself another glass of wine. Finally, she took a seat on his couch, raised her glass, and said, "Welcome to parenthood."

CHAPTER 22

"Are you okay with stopping at Dad's?" Abby asked Yvette as they cruised by the river that ran through town.

"Absolutely. We need to check on him anyway and make sure he's taking it easy. Did you know he'd started treatments again?" Yvette asked as the golf cart puttered along at the top speed of eighteen miles an hour.

"No." Abby scowled. "Do you know why he passed out? Was it the chemotherapy or something else?"

"He just overdid it and let himself get dehydrated, that's all."

"Right." She turned down the road that led to their childhood home. "I'm positive it's because he ran out of the energy potion I was making for him, and he didn't want to ask me to make more right before the wedding. Then he continued to push his limits anyway. Can you believe him?"

Unfortunately, Yvette could believe her father would do such a thing. He'd always been the one they all leaned on. Now that he had to lean on them, he was having trouble accepting his new circumstances. "Yes. He's a stubborn old bird."

"Okay, tell me what happened," Abby said.

"When dad passed out? He was in his office and—"

"No. I already heard about all of that. I mean what happened to provoke this emergency golf cart ride."

Yvette shrugged, suddenly not at all interested in talking about Jacob. The image of him with Sienna and their child was making her nauseated.

"Vette, come on. Something happened. You need to spill; otherwise, I'm going to just start guessing. Like did you walk into the coffee shop and find Isaac groping Jake? Or did you lose a cash deposit on the way to the bank, and now the shop is in danger of going under? How about you hit on a twenty-two-year-old college guy in the department store, and his mother happened to be a few feet away picking out his new underwear?"

Yvette let out a bark of laughter. "No, no, and oh my goddess, that would've been hilarious, but no. Not even close."

"So, it really doesn't have anything to do with Isaac?" she asked, her expression serious now.

"No, nothing like that." Yvette took a deep breath. "Okay, you've been gone for the past two weeks, so you've missed a lot."

"Noel filled me in on some things, like how you took Clay's friend home with you the night of the wedding." She pumped her eyebrows then glanced at Yvette's abdomen. "Oh, jeez. You're not pregnant, are you? Tell me you used protection."

Yvette rolled her eyes. "No, I'm not pregnant, and yes, protection was used."

"Okay, that's good. One crisis averted anyway." Abby grinned at her sister. "I also hear that Jacob is your new business partner. Is that the problem? Has he decided he can't keep his hands off you, and now you're stuck with fending off a gorgeous guy on a daily basis? I mean, I can see how that could get annoying after a while."

"Uh, well, I wouldn't put it like that, but we did sort of start something."

"Oh? Are you two getting it on in the stacks at the bookstore?" Abby teased.

"Good goddess, Abby. Is this what you and Clay did on your honeymoon? Get in on in public all over the place?"

She giggled. "No, but there was this one night when—"

"Never mind. I don't think I want to hear this," Yvette said. "If you must know, Jacob and I only had the one night together, and then we were trying to keep it professional."

"I'm guessing that didn't last?" Abby asked as she turned down the long drive to their dad's house.

"No. Not long at all. By the end of the first week, we'd decided to go ahead and officially start dating. But then he went to L.A. to finalize some paperwork with his ex, and he came back all moody. After a few days, we were right back on track and then today—" Yvette's voice cracked on the word today, and she took a moment to collect herself. "Today his ex showed up with a baby. Jacob's baby."

Abby's eyes went wide. "He has a kid?"

"Apparently, only he never told me that, even after we talked about how our exes had really messed us up. I just don't know why he hid her from me. He doesn't even have pictures of her in his house. Honestly, Abby, it completely threw me for a loop."

Abby glanced over at her sister. "Maybe he's just wary of letting anyone new into his daughter's life. You know, maybe he just wants to protect her and doesn't want to rush anything when it comes to her."

Yvette could see Abby's point. If she had a child, she'd be really careful about introducing them to someone she was dating. Things would have to be really serious. Except… "Abs, he didn't even tell me about her. And she's still a baby. It's not like she'd get attached to me and be confused about who I am in her dad's life. I just… it hurt that he didn't trust me enough to tell me."

Abby reached over and grabbed her sister's hand, squeezing it lightly. "You probably should just talk to him about it. I'm sure he has his reasons."

"Right." Yvette scowled. "Except right now his ex is at his house for the weekend, and all I can think about is going over there and… well, I don't know what I would do, but I hate the idea that they are together. Who knows what they're doing?"

Abby shook her head at her sister. "Yeah, I'm sure it's real romantic changing diapers and pureeing baby food."

"Well, when you put it that way," Yvette said, "this ride on the golf cart does sound a hundred percent more enjoyable."

"Stick with me, baby! I know how to party."

Abby rounded the curve and the house came into view.

Yvette muttered a curse and wondered how her day could get any worse.

"Oh, yikes. Is that Isaac's new BMW?" Abby asked, eyeing the black roadster in Lin's driveway.

"Yep. He apparently bought it because it's Jake's dream car," she said with a sigh.

"We can come back later," Abby said, already turning the cart around.

"No. It's fine. Let's go in. I want to see Dad, too."

"Are you sure?" Abby asked. "No one expects you to interact with your ex-husband."

"I'm sure," Yvette said. "He still does work for Dad. I'm going to have to get used to it sometime."

Abby gave her a skeptical look but pulled the cart to a stop anyway. "Okay, but if he makes you want to murder someone, just give me the signal and we'll get out of here ASAP. Got it?"

"You're a good sister." Yvette hopped out of the cart, scowled at the Roadster, and strode into the house, determined to not let Isaac drive her away from her family home. The log-cabin-style house was a large, rambling one story, yet it felt cozy and welcoming with the fire crackling in the hearth. A large metal pentacle hung over the fireplace, signifying their connection to the witch community, and there were candles everywhere, though they weren't lit. Yvette snapped her fingers and they all flamed to life.

Lin Townsend looked up from his spot at the table and grinned at his two daughters. "Well, isn't this a surprise?"

"Hi, Dad," Yvette said. Then she gave Isaac, who was sitting across from Lin, a curt nod.

"Hi, Dad," Abby echoed and ran over to give him a hug. "I missed you."

"You were only gone two weeks. That's hardly enough time to be missing your old man," he said, but he held her hand with both of his as he dismissed her statement.

"Of course it is, silly," she said and gave him a kiss on the cheek. "I brought your energy potions. Want to help me unload them from the cart?"

"Sure." The two of them wandered back outside, leaving Yvette and Isaac alone.

"Looks like you're enjoying the new car," Yvette said as she moved to the kitchen to grab a cup of coffee.

Isaac didn't respond to her comment but stood and followed her into the kitchen. "Yvette?"

"What?" she asked without turning around.

"I owe you an apology."

She froze. Yvette knew him well enough to know that this apology, whatever it was for, wasn't easy for him. The quiet way he'd said it gave him away. She glanced over her shoulder. "For what?"

"For trying to interfere with the way you run the bookstore. Jake said—"

"I'm not interested in anything Jake has to say," Yvette said, anger filling her up and making her want to haul off and hit something, preferably him.

"Yvette, please, just hear me out, and then you'll never have to talk to me again if you don't want to."

She let out an incredulous huff. "Really, Isaac? You work for my dad and we both live in this very small town. I don't think never talking is really in the cards."

"Then we should do our best to form a truce. What do you say?"

Yvette gritted her teeth and turned around. "I'm not at war with you, Isaac. I just can't have you acting like we're still married. You have no right to tell me how to live my life or how to run my business. I'm a big girl. I've got it covered."

"I know." He very gently took her by the hand and led her back to the table. "Please, have a seat."

She was tempted to tell him no and stalk right out of there, but she had to admit that she was more than a little curious about what he was going to say. Without comment, she seated herself and waited.

He pulled a chair up so that he was sitting right in front of her. Then he took both of her hands in his and said, "I'm so very sorry for how I treated you, Yvette."

"You told me this at the wedding two weeks ago," she said, unimpressed with his constant apologies. He'd turned her life upside down and treated her like she was too incompetent to run her own bookstore. "Unless there's more, I think we're done here."

His grip tightened on hers, and his eyes sparkled with

unshed tears. "I've been so selfish. You deserved better. I know you don't want to hear about Jake, but he's the one who helped me see what a jackass I've been." Isaac blinked, and the tears cleared. "I know the bookstore is yours, and I had no business sticking my nose in where it didn't belong."

"No, you really didn't," she said, unsure what to make of this apology. She had heard it before, but this time his sincerity seemed much more authentic, as if he really did understand how he'd been hurting her and wanted to make it right instead of just easing his own guilt for leaving their marriage.

"Congratulations, by the way. I heard the signing was a huge success." He flashed her his gorgeous grin, making her remember one of the reasons she'd fallen in love with him in the first place.

"Thank you. It was a team effort."

"I'm sure you're being modest," he said. "You always did understand how to get customers in the store and move books."

"Well, thanks."

"I've just been having a hard time letting go. And then I saw you with Jacob, and I guess I got jealous."

She raised her eyebrows. "Why? What does it matter if I date someone new?"

"Come on, Yvette," he said giving her a pained look. "I married you because I loved you. That wasn't a lie, you know."

A dull ache throbbed in her chest, but it was a far cry from the piercing pain she'd had when he'd told her he was leaving. "I know."

"Do you?" he asked earnestly. "Do you really understand how hard it was for me?"

She stared at him. She had placed herself in his shoes many times before, trying to see his perspective. It hadn't eased the pain, but she did understand the turmoil he must've faced when he realized he'd been living a lie. "Yes, but that doesn't change how I feel about it… or felt anyway. Listen, Isaac, we don't have to keep doing this. Let's just try to respect each other, and maybe one day we'll get back to being the friends we were before we became romantically involved. Does that sound fair?"

He nodded. "Completely fair. I just hope that day is sooner rather than later. I know it isn't fair for me to say this, but I miss you."

Her eyes misted, and she squeezed his hands just as he'd done a moment before. "I miss you, too. I don't think you understand how hard it was for me to lose my husband and my best friend."

"I think I do. I lost you, too, you know."

She frowned. "But you had Jake to fill the void. Who did I have? And don't say my sisters or my dad because it isn't the same."

"Jake could never replace you," he said, and something in his tone made her believe him.

"Thanks for that," she said, one tear rolling down her cheek.

Isaac stood and pulled her to her feet. Then he wrapped his arms around her and said, "I'll always love you, Yvette. I hope you know that."

A sob got caught in her throat, and she nodded, feeling for the first time that maybe she hadn't lost him, that maybe, just maybe, they could find their way back to being friends again.

"Hey, now what's going on in here? Isaac, are you making my daughter cry again?" Lin asked as he strode into the room with Abby on his heels. "I told you that if you ever hurt her again, you'd have to answer to me."

Isaac kissed Yvette's cheek and said, "Unfortunately, I think I did make her cry, Lin. I apologize."

"Dammit, now I'm going to have to fire you," he said,

glaring at Isaac. "I should've done it after you broke her heart the first time. What is wrong with you, man?"

"Dad," Yvette said, wiping her eyes. "You can't fire Isaac. Who's going to do your books?"

"We'll find someone else. Maybe Jacob can take over," he said stubbornly.

Yvette chuckled. "Jacob can read a financial statement just fine, but he's no bookkeeper. I think it's best for the business if we stick with Isaac here. Besides, I'm fine. Isaac and I were just making up, that's all."

"You were?" Lin eyed them carefully then frowned. "Does this mean Jake is history?"

Isaac cleared his throat. "Um, no."

"Then I don't get it. You're not implying the three of you are going to be involved—"

"Dad!" Yvette shouted. "Oh, my goddess, no. I meant we're going to try to be friends again. That's all."

"Oh. Well thank the gods." He turned to Isaac. "My Yvette deserves to be the one and only in someone's life."

"I couldn't agree more." Isaac started to pick up a file he'd left on the table. "I should go."

"Not yet," Yvette said. "Abby and I are taking the golf cart out for a spin. Why don't you join us?"

"Really?" Isaac asked, surprise in his hopeful eyes.

"Really." She turned to Lin. "You, too, Dad. It's time for you to have some fun."

"No way," Lin said. "Have you seen how Abby drives that thing? I'd be taking my life in my hands."

"Come on, Dad," Abby chimed in from her spot near the fireplace. "You just told me you didn't want to end up locked in the house all the time. Come for a ride with us. I'll be careful."

"No, she won't," Yvette said. "But you should come anyway. How bad can it be? The cart only goes eighteen miles an hour."

"Come on, Lin," Isaac said. "Your girls are waiting."

"Fine," Lin muttered. "But if something goes wrong, I'll never let you forget it."

Abby snorted. "No doubt."

"Excellent," Yvette said. "Now if only we had another cart, we could have golf cart races."

Lin cleared his throat. "Well, now that you mention it, we just might be in luck."

Both Abby and Yvette turned and stared at him.

"What do you mean?" Yvette asked.

Lin jerked his head. "Follow me."

The three of them did as they were told and soon found themselves in Lin's garage staring at a brand-new black golf cart.

"Dad?" Abby said with a laugh. "Where did this come from?"

"I bought it," he said proudly, shoving the key into the ignition. "Check this out." He flicked a switch, and the golf cart lit up with flashing red twinkle lights while a sound system started playing "On the Road Again" by Willie Nelson.

Abby threw her head back and laughed. "Dad, this is fantastic."

"This is your influence," Yvette said to her sister, referring to the fact that Abby's golf cart had the same features.

"Gosh, I certainly hope so." Abby turned to her father. "So, Dad, what brought this on? Not that I don't approve, because obviously I do."

He shrugged. "I figured I could use something to help me get around the orchard. This was a lot more fun than a utility cart."

"You got that right." Abby pointed at the cart. "You ready to race, old man?"

"You read my mind," he said and climbed in behind the wheel.

Yvette grinned at her dad, pride making her swell with love for him. There was only one reason he'd gotten that cart—so he wouldn't have to wear himself out walking the property. He was really trying to take it easy and was doing it in style.

"I'm with Dad!" Yvette jumped in beside him. "Ready to kick Abby's butt?"

He eyed Abby. "Do you think we can take her?"

"Definitely. Your driving skills are far superior."

"Oh ho! You think so, huh?" Abby waved at Isaac. "Come on, Isaac. We need to talk strategy so we can leave these two in the dust."

"Is there such a thing as strategy when it comes to a golf cart?" Isaac asked her as they strode out of the garage and over to her cart.

"Not usually, but I have some tricks up my sleeve." Abby glanced over her shoulder. "Watch out, you two. I wouldn't want you to get caught in my dust storm."

"Right." Lin eased the cart down to the end of the driveway. Then he turned to Yvette. "What should we do? Wait for her or just go for it?"

"Go for it," Yvette urged as Abby climbed into her cart. "Now!"

Lin stomped on the gas and they jerked forward.

"Hey! That's cheating," Abby called from behind them.

Yvette reached over to the volume button as she glanced at her father. He nodded once and with his approval, Yvette turned up her father's country music, drowning out Abby's cries of protest.

Lin tapped his left foot and bounced his fingers on the steering wheel. His body was relaxed, and his color was normal. There was no question he was taking better care of himself. She wanted to tell him she was proud of him, but instead, she just reached over and lightly squeezed his shoulder.

He glanced over at her.

Thank you, she mouthed.

"Anything for my girls!" he shouted over the music. Then he took a hard right turn toward the enchanted river. A few moments later, Abby's golf cart appeared beside them and the race was on.

Yvette leaned forward in the cart and yelled encouragement for her dad to outpace Abby, screaming and shouting the entire way, loving every minute of it.

In the end, Lin lost the race, but Yvette knew it was because Abby's cart was outfitted with boosters and other performance-enhancing equipment. There'd been almost no chance of eking out a win, but that wasn't what mattered to Yvette.

As she watched her sister and Isaac do a complicated and completely ridiculous victory dance, the only thing she cared about was how much fun she was having with them and her dad. The pure joy she felt filled all the empty spaces in her heart. This was what family was about and why she loved Keating Hollow with her entire heart and soul.

CHAPTER 23

Wednesday morning rolled around, and Jacob found himself with Skye strapped to his chest while he slipped into Incantation Café. Because Skye had cried half the night, he'd had less than four hours of sleep the night before and his eyes were watering from fatigue, but he didn't care. He'd completely and utterly fallen in love with his daughter. And he knew that he'd happily forgo the next eighteen years of sleep if it meant he got to spend that time with her.

"Oh my," Hanna said as Jacob approached the counter. "Who is this precious little girl?"

"My daughter, Skye," he said, pride coloring his tone.

"She's beautiful, Jacob. I didn't know you had a daughter." Hanna held her finger out to the little girl and grinned when Skye wrapped her hand around it and held on tight. "And strong, too."

Jacob almost said he hadn't known either, but he kept that to himself and just smiled at Hanna as she cooed at his daughter.

Finally, Hanna glanced up. "Coffee? Large?"

"The largest, thanks."

"You got it."

Jacob put a few bills on the counter and stepped back just as the front door opened and another customer stepped into the shop. There was a tiny, surprised gasp, and he instantly knew Yvette was behind him. He turned and saw her standing there, staring at him with her mouth open. He smiled at her. "Hi."

She cleared her throat. "Hi."

He hadn't seen her since Friday when Sienna had interrupted their lunch. He'd called to let her know he wouldn't be coming into the bookstore. He'd wanted to explain, but she'd cut him off, said she understood, and ended the call. He'd considered calling back but decided the conversation would be better in person.

Hanna called his name and handed him his coffee. Then she turned to Yvette. "Latte?"

Yvette nodded. The expression on her face as she stared at Jacob and Skye was a mix of interest and something that vaguely resembled fear as if she was ready to bolt at any minute.

Jacob added cream and sugar to his coffee then moved to stand next to Yvette. "We need to talk."

"No, we don't. It's fine. Your daughter is here. You should spend as much time as possible with her. I've got the bookstore covered." She gave him a too bright smile and glanced away.

"Yvette, I—"

The door swung open, and Sienna walked in. She was wearing formfitting jeans, knee high stiletto boots and a low-cut sweater that showed off her impressive cleavage. Jacob had wondered where exactly she thought she was going when she'd emerged from her bedroom this morning. It was an outfit she was likely to wear to the morning talk shows her publicist arranged to promote Enchanted Bliss. "There you are. I just got off the phone with my assistant. She's gotten our flights arranged for Friday morning at seven."

Yvette gaped at her then turned her gaze on Jacob. "You're leaving?"

A lump formed in Jacob's throat when he saw the devastated look on Yvette's face. This wasn't at all how he'd wanted to tell her. "Like I said, we need to talk."

"Oh, you didn't know?" Sienna asked with fake sincerity. "That's too bad. I guess you're pretty upset that Jacob won't be around to turn that little bookstore of yours into a successful franchise. He's *really* good at that sort of thing."

Yvette glared at her. "I think I'll manage."

Sienna shrugged and walked over to the counter.

"I guess this means you two are giving it another try?" Yvette asked Jacob while continuing to glare at Sienna.

"What?" Jacob blinked then frowned. "No. *No*, not at all." He glanced down at the little girl wiggling in her pack. "I'm going because of her."

Realization dawned in Yvette's eyes, and everything about her softened. She gazed at Skye and very softly said, "I see."

"Do you have time to talk today?" he asked, his eyes pleading with her. "There are things to say."

Her eyes glistened with tears, but she held them back as she shook her head. "Listen, Jacob, it's really okay. I understand. There's no reason to—"

"I have things to say," he said stubbornly. "Just give me a half hour if for nothing other than to work out things with the bookstore."

She hesitated and opened her mouth, but then she closed it and nodded. "I'll be at the store all day. Just come by before we close."

"I'll be there in an hour."

"Yvette?" Hanna called. "Your latte is ready."

Jacob stared down at her intently, his insides churning with regret. He'd missed her the past five days. Living with Sienna hadn't been any picnic, and it made him appreciate the kind creature in front of him even more than he had before. She was so real and open and loving. Before he'd moved to Keating Hollow, he hadn't known what he wanted. He did now, and Yvette was the only one for him.

"Come on, Jacob," Sienna said, slipping her arm through his. "We need to get back if we're going to keep that appointment with the realtor."

"Realtor?" Yvette asked, alarm flashing in her blue eyes. "You're selling your house?"

Jacob tried to swallow the lump in his throat as he nodded. "I'll need the resources if I want to move to Aspen."

YVETTE SAT at her desk staring blankly at the computer screen. The moment she found out Jacob was leaving, her heart had broken in two. It hadn't even been a month since she'd first met him, but she'd fallen so completely in love with him that she wasn't sure she was ever going to be the same once he left town. Add in the fact that he was selling his house, and she was positive she'd never see him again. Sure, they owned the bookstore together, but the truth was she didn't need him around to manage the day to day operations, and anything she required of him could be taken care of by email.

The door cracked open and heavy footsteps sounded on her wood floors. She knew it was him, but she was afraid if she looked up and saw him she'd start to cry. Then she heard the sweet sound of a baby giggle.

She was doomed. Yvette glanced up at Jacob's handsome face and saw regret shining back at her. "No," she said, shaking her head. "Don't do that. I don't think I can take it."

"Do what? Leave town? I don't really have much of a choice," he said, coming to a stop just on the other side of her desk.

"No, I mean look at me like that." She shifted her gaze to the sweet baby girl he was holding. She was waving her arms as she tried to reach for Yvette. Her heart melted into a big pile of goo. Yvette held her hands out toward the baby. "May I?"

His expression softened as he handed his daughter to Yvette. "Of course."

The little girl had a fresh baby scent that made Yvette sigh with pleasure. "She's perfect, Jacob."

He stuffed his hands in his pockets and nodded. "I can't say I disagree with you."

Yvette sat back down in her chair and made faces at Skye. The baby giggled happily. Finally, Yvette glanced at Jacob. "Why didn't you tell me about her?"

Jacob took a seat and leaned forward. "Because I didn't even know she existed until I went down to Los Angeles to meet with Sienna. She told me she thought Skye was Brian's, but then a blood test proved she's mine." He glanced at his daughter, the love in his eyes palpable. When he glanced back up and met Yvette's gaze, he added, "I was pretty messed up by the news. It took me a few days to figure out how to even deal with it, and that's why I was distant when I got back."

She took a deep breath. "I can see how that came as quite the shock."

"That's an understatement." Jacob explained how Sienna was supposed to bring Skye up for the weekend for him to meet her and then decided Jacob needed more time with his daughter, so she extended the trip. "That's why she's still here.

I'd already decided I would probably have to move so I could be near Skye, I just hadn't made up my mind. After these past few days, there's no question. I just have to, Yvette."

She eyed the sweet little girl and could only imagine what he must be feeling. His love for her was already a shining beacon every time he looked at her. The fact he'd fallen so hard and so fast only made Yvette love him more. "As much as I don't want you to go, I completely understand."

He sat back in the chair and just gazed at her. "You do know that if it weren't for Skye, absolutely nothing could drag me away from Keating Hollow, right?"

"You did say you've always loved the town," she said with a tiny shrug.

"That's not why." He stood and rounded the desk. He leaned against the edge and reached out, caressing her cheek. "Before I went to L.A. the only thing I wanted to do was spend more time with you. And maybe it's cruel to tell you this when I have no choice but to leave, but I was going to do everything in my power to make you fall for me, too."

"*Too*? Are you trying to tell me you wanted something more than just a few make out sessions?"

He laughed. "Much, much more, Yvette. I think I'm always going to regret not finding out where this thing with us was going. You'll be the one who got away… unless you come with me."

Her entire body stiffened. "Did you just ask me to move to Aspen with you?"

This time his laugh was full of nervous energy. "I guess maybe I did. It's way too soon, isn't it?"

"It's… yes, way too soon," she said sadly. "Even if we leave out the fact that I have a bookstore to run, I *just* got divorced, my family is here, and Keating Hollow is my home. And you…" She ran a light hand over Skye's curls. "You need to figure out your place in this little one's life without me getting in the way. Maybe someday in the future we'll find our way back to each other, but right now I think it's best for both of us to take a step back."

He was silent as an array of emotions flittered over his face, but when his gaze landed on his daughter again, he nodded. "You're right. It's about her now."

"She's really lucky, you know. You're going to be the best dad she could ever ask for."

"I hope so." He tugged Yvette out of her chair and stepped in close, holding her with one arm, his daughter still between them. "Tell me it isn't just me. Tell me that you feel this, too."

Tears glittered in her eyes as she whispered, "I feel it, too."

"This isn't the end of us, Yvette Townsend. Not if I have anything to say about it." He leaned in and brushed his lips over hers.

Yvette clutched at him, knowing that with time and distance his feelings were likely to change. But still, she clung to the hope that he was correct and someday they'd have their chance. Her throat started to ache with the tears she was holding at bay and she pulled back, handing Skye to him. "You should go before this gets any harder."

He took his daughter and said, "About the bookstore... since I won't be here, I'll become your silent partner. I'll have Norm send over the new paperwork."

"What?" A cold dread washed over her. She'd accepted that he was leaving, but in the back of her mind she'd been counting on the fact that she'd still be in touch with him on a regular basis about the store. "You don't have to do that. We can talk by phone or email."

"I know I don't have to, but I don't want you to feel like I'm second guessing your decisions. Of course, I'll be available if you want to bounce anything off me. I was just trying to be fair to you."

She shook her head. "Absolutely not. I like your input, and we work well together. Leave everything the way it is."

"Okay, then." He smiled at her and started to lean in again, but the door burst open and Sienna stumbled in.

"Jacob, we have to go. Now!"

CHAPTER 24

Jacob jerked back from Yvette, still holding Skye close to him. "What's wrong?"

"It's Brian. He's here in Keating Hollow," she said on a sob. "He's been looking for you. You have to get out of here."

Jacob frowned at her. "Why is he looking for me? We don't have anything to say to each other."

Sienna grabbed his hand and started tugging him toward the door. "He's pissed about us living together. Come on. Hurry before he finds us and beats the crap out of you."

"First of all, I'm not afraid of Brian. Second, we're not living together, and he has nothing to worry about where you and I are concerned," Jacob said, planting his feet. "What did you tell him?"

"The truth." Tears started streaming down her face, and she kept glancing at the door as if she expected Brian to burst in at any moment.

"Perhaps you two should be alone for this discussion?" Yvette said and slipped past Jacob, heading for the door.

"Oh no you don't, you evil witch." Sienna grabbed Yvette's arm and yanked her back. "I know you seduced my fiancé. Did you think I was going to just let that go?"

Shocked by Sienna's outburst, Jacob was momentarily speechless. But he quickly found his voice as Yvette turned accusing eyes on him. He said, "I don't know what she's talking about. Sienna is definitely *not* my fiancée."

"Maybe not technically," Sienna said as she gazed up at him and batted her eyelashes. "But now that you know we share a daughter, I'm sure we will be engaged again soon enough."

Jacob frowned. "Have you lost your mind?"

Yvette stared at Sienna's hand clutching her arm, and in a low, barely controlled voice she said, "You should let go of me now before I make you."

Sienna tightened her grip on Yvette's arm.

"Sienna!" Jacob scolded. "What are you doing?"

She jumped back as if startled he was still there. Then she ran up to him. "Please, let's go."

"Maybe you should take her home," Yvette said. "She seems… upset."

"That's one way of putting it." Jacob adjusted Skye, getting a better hold on her, and then he turned his attention back to Sienna. "Okay, let's go and get out of Yvette's way."

Sienna started to walk toward the door, but then she turned back and glared at Yvette. "He's mine. Don't even think about trying to seduce him again."

Anger burned through Jacob, and he wanted nothing more than to throttle Sienna. How had she even known he'd been with Yvette? He certainly hadn't told her. "That's enough, Sienna," he warned. "I don't know what game you're playing, but it stops right now, got it?"

"I'm not playing games, sweetheart," she purred, stroking his arm. "I'm just trying to keep my family together."

"I'm not your family." He cast Yvette a pained expression. His face burned with heat over Sienna's freak show performance. He had no idea where this manic, crazed person had come from. For the past five days, she'd been normal enough. And while she'd been relatively self-absorbed, that wasn't exactly new behavior. Whatever was going on now was a completely different thing.

"But we are family, Jake," Sienna said sweetly, using the nickname he'd always hated. "You'll see. Once you get to Aspen and see the place I've chosen for us, you'll see things my way."

"I highly doubt that," he muttered. He glanced over his shoulder at Yvette and mouthed, *I'll call you later.*

She nodded once and sank back down in her chair, looking shell-shocked by hurricane Sienna. He couldn't blame her. Sienna's outbursts were enough to make him question her sanity.

"Sienna!" a man called from the front of the bookshop in a voice Jacob would recognize anywhere.

Brian.

Jacob paused, wondering if Sienna hadn't just been causing unnecessary drama when she'd warned him that Brian wanted a piece of him. He straightened his shoulders, tightened his hold on Skye and strode out into the bookstore with Sienna pleading for him to go out the back door.

"Sienna!" he said harshly. "I'm not running away from Brian."

The moment Jacob spotted Brian, rage filtered through his entire body. His best friend, the one guy he'd considered his brother, had run off with his fiancée and never looked back. He felt himself tense, and he glanced back at Sienna. "Here, take Skye."

"No!" She waved her hands in front of her face and darted off to the side. "She's your baby!"

"What? You're her mother. Stop this, Sienna. Take her so I can talk to Brian."

"I wouldn't do that if I were you," Brian said, staring at Sienna. "She's not… stable."

"Here, I'll take her," Yvette said quietly from right behind him.

Relieved she was there, he turned and handed her Skye. "Thank you."

"Sure." Yvette carefully cradled the baby and moved over toward the café, probably trying to put as much distance between them as possible in case there actually was some sort of altercation.

"What exactly do you mean by 'not stable'?" Jacob asked Brian.

His old friend sighed. "Have you really not noticed anything different about her?"

Jacob studied Sienna, saw her wild eyes and her fidgety hands. He recalled her being a little off during the last five days, muttering to herself and hiding in the guest room while he took care of Skye, but he'd thought she was just stressed over the situation and was giving him time to get to know his daughter. But after the rantings she'd spewed in Yvette's office, he couldn't disagree with Brian's assessment. She clearly *wasn't* stable. "She seems to think you're here to throw down with me or something. You're not, are you?"

"What do you think?" Brian strode over to Sienna who was now curled in one of the overstuffed chairs, sobbing about how she'd ruined her life and that no one would ever love her again.

"No, I don't think so," Jacob said, watching in awe as Brian gently lifted Sienna out of the chair. He cradled her in his arms and whispered, "You're okay now, Sienna. I'm here. I'm not going to let anything happen to you. Everything is going to be all right now."

Jacob's insides went cold. When he'd said she wasn't stable, he wasn't just referring to a temporary freak out. Sienna was sick and clearly needed help. He instantly felt like the biggest jackass who'd ever lived. "When did this start?"

Brian glanced up. "Not long after she left you. Probably before that, but no one could see it yet. I didn't, and neither did her mother."

Guilt ate away at Jacob's gut. "I didn't know." He wanted to walk over to Sienna and lend a soothing hand, but she was curled up in Brian's arms, resting her head on his shoulder. Clearly neither of them needed Jacob's help.

"I'm going to get her to the healer," Brian said. "I'll come by after and explain everything."

Jacob didn't know what to do or say, so he just nodded. But as Brian started to move toward the front door, Jacob blurted out, "Is it true that Skye is my daughter, or was all of that a lie, too?"

Brian glanced over at Yvette and Skye. Pain flashed in his tortured eyes for just a moment before his expression cleared. Then he looked Jacob right in the eye and said, "She's definitely yours, brother."

As a rush of relief flooded Jacob's body, he watched Brian stoically carry Sienna out of the store.

"Jacob?" Yvette said quietly from behind him.

"Yeah?" He was still staring at the door, completely gutted and not at all sure of how he was supposed to feel about what had just gone down.

"Are you okay?" she asked.

He shook his head. "No, not at all."

"That's okay. Come on. Let's get out of here." She slipped one hand in his and started leading him out of the store.

"Where are we going?" he asked, still stupefied by the day's events.

"Home."

CHAPTER 25

Jacob sat in the passenger seat of Yvette's Mustang and marveled at the woman beside him. She'd somehow gotten the baby seat out of Sienna's rental, transferred it to her car, and secured Skye in the back. Then she'd coaxed him into the passenger seat, and he couldn't even remember any of it. By the time he returned to the land of the living, they were winding their way up the side of the mountain to his house.

"Thank you," he said.

"There's no need for that." She smiled softly at him. "I'm just doing what any friend would do after the day you've had."

"You must have some really good friends." He glanced into the back seat at his daughter and was comforted to see her sleeping peacefully.

"You know, I do. And so do you."

He let out a sardonic laugh. "You just saw my friends. It's possible I need new ones."

"Well, you've got me." She pulled her Mustang into his driveway and put the car in park. "And while things may be rocky with you and Brian, I think he's probably a better friend than you're giving him credit for."

"Maybe," Jacob said begrudgingly. Sienna *had* told him that Brian had been the one who'd insisted she come clean about Skye's paternity. Judging by the way he'd looked at the little girl, that couldn't have been easy for him if he'd first believed she was his child.

"I guess you'll find out when he gets here." Yvette climbed out of the car, and by the time she met him on the passenger side, he'd already freed Skye from the back seat.

Yvette led the way into his house, and while he was busy putting the baby down in the portable crib, she disappeared into the kitchen. After he was done changing and soothing his daughter, he met her in the kitchen and felt an overwhelming rush of gratitude as he watched her fix them dinner.

"I didn't know if you were hungry, but I figured either way you're going to need fuel." She set a plate with a sandwich and a pile of chips in front of him and another one next to it.

Jacob sat on the stool and pulled her down to sit in his lap. "Thank you again."

She pressed her hand to his cheek. "I'm just doing what friends do."

"No, Yvette. This isn't what my friends do. They've never done this. I'm grateful and overwhelmed, and I want to kiss you so bad right now it hurts."

Her lips curved into a small smile. "Then kiss me."

He cupped her cheek, caressing her cheekbone with his thumb. Then he leaned in and tenderly pressed his lips to hers. Emotion flooded him, and he poured every bit of himself into the kiss as he wrapped his arms around her and held her close.

Her hands tightened on his shoulders as she matched his intensity, giving herself over to him. They caressed and kissed and held each other. Jacob would've gladly stayed locked in her embrace for as long as she'd have him, but all too soon there was a knock on his door.

"Damn. I wasn't finished here," he whispered as he broke away. They were both a little winded and a lot worked up.

"It has to be Brian," she said. And just like that, the spell that had fallen over them was broken.

"Right." He gently nudged her off his lap and got up to answer the door.

Brian stood on the porch with his shoulders hunched and his back to Jacob as he stared out over the forest. Jacob stepped outside and joined him.

"Where's Sienna?" Jacob asked.

"She's with the healer in town. I'll pick her up later and take her back to L.A. where her mother is," Brian said, still staring out at the view.

"Not Aspen?"

"No. She'll need to wait until there's another opening at the clinic."

Jacob frowned. "What clinic? Don't you two live there?"

Brian turned to Jacob, his brow furrowed in confusion. "What gave you that idea?"

"She told me you two were opening an Enchanted Bliss flagship location and that you were moving there permanently."

"Oh, man." Brian ran a hand through his black hair and sighed. "She's really off the rails this time."

"So there's no store in Aspen, and you definitely don't live there?" Jacob asked.

"No store. And we don't live there, or at least I don't."

"Okay, I think you'd better just start at the beginning, because clearly I have no idea what's going on," Jacob said. "Were you and Sienna together?"

Brian glanced at him, his face pinched. "Yes. Once after a drunken night when you were out of town."

Jacob's stomach turned. This was the first time he'd heard the truth straight from his best friend's lips. "Just once?"

He swallowed. "Just once while you were still together."

"I see. Maybe we better go inside," Jacob said. "I'll put a pot of coffee on and we can go from there."

Brian nodded, and Jacob led the way into his house. Jacob started a pot of coffee and when Yvette appeared, he introduced her to his friend and made it clear that anything Brian had to say, he could say in front of her.

"All right," Brian said.

After a few awkward minutes, the coffee was done and the three of them sat at Jacob's table.

Brian cleared his throat and pierced Jacob with his steady gaze. "I just have to know one thing—did you know she's sick?"

"Who? Sienna?" Jacob frowned. "What do you mean exactly?"

"Her mental state, Jacob. Did you know?" he asked.

"Did I know she's unstable? No, I never guessed until today when she came in ranting about you and insisting I run out the back door. I never saw her behave that way while we were together. How long has this been going on?"

He shrugged. "I don't know exactly. She can be good at hiding it as long as no one questions the lies she tells."

Jacob felt the guilt crawl up the back of his throat. He'd never questioned Sienna on much of anything. It wasn't what he wanted in a partner. She'd been free to go anywhere, see anyone, or buy anything she wanted without input from him. He'd never cared. But maybe that was the problem. He just hadn't cared enough to realize there was one.

Brian wrapped his hands around his coffee mug, and while staring at the dark liquid, he said, "I owe you an apology,

Jacob." He glanced up, anguish lining his features. "That night with Sienna was a huge mistake. I knew it as soon as it was over and honestly, I wanted to pretend it had never happened."

"But?" Jacob prompted.

"Sienna, she kept coming around, telling me how your relationship was falling apart and that she needed me to help her get out of it before you two got married. I kept telling her to just talk to you. She said she had but things were just getting worse. She had me believing you two were sleeping in separate bedrooms." He took a sip of the coffee and set the cup back down on the table. "Then she came to me and said she was pregnant and there was no way it wasn't mine."

Yvette, who'd been as quiet as a church mouse since she'd taken a seat at the table, let out a tiny gasp.

Brian glanced at her. "Exactly. Up until six weeks ago, I was convinced Skye was my daughter."

"Son of a..." Jacob closed his eyes and felt the other man's pain slice through him. "Sienna said you were the one who urged her to get in contact with me. Is that true?"

He nodded, keeping his eyes averted. "She's your daughter. You had to know."

Jacob felt his eyes burn with emotion, but he didn't let the tears fall. His voice was hoarse and barely audible when he forced out, "Thank you for that."

Brian was silent for a long moment. Then he cleared his throat again and continued to explain everything that had happened. After Sienna had told Brian she was pregnant with his baby, he'd promised to be there for her; that he'd get her anything she needed; and that he'd be by her side through the entire process. At first, she'd seemed completely normal. But then as the pregnancy wore on, her behavior became more and more bizarre.

"I told her she had to start seeing a professional," Brian said.

"So she started seeing someone in Los Angeles. She was doing okay for a while, but after Skye was born, she was in bad shape. Postpartum combined with her other issues landed her in a facility in Aspen. That's probably why she said we were opening a store there."

"Goodness, the poor thing," Yvette said. "That sounds rough."

Brian nodded. "She came back to L.A. about a month ago. She was better, but not 'cured.' She's still in therapy and supposed to be taking mood stabilizers."

"I assume she's not taking her meds then," Jacob said.

"Apparently not. At least that's what she told the healer. Anyway, by the time Sienna returned home, I'd already realized that Skye wasn't mine. And I swear, I really did consider contacting you, but I needed to talk to Sienna first. She admitted that she'd lied to me about you and a host of other things. When the smoke cleared, she wanted to be the one to tell you about Skye. And because she had been making good progress, the therapist thought it was a good idea. She knows she isn't well, Jacob. It's important that you know she only wants what's best for Skye."

"Is that why she was trying to get me to sell my house and move to a city where you two don't live?" he asked, unable to control his frustration.

"I'm going to assume she did that because she loves her daughter and doesn't want to lose her," he said, sounding irritated and protective at the same time.

"Because she's afraid I'm going to sue for custody," Jacob said, filling in the blanks.

"No, brother. That's not it at all. Sienna has her faults, but when it comes to the love of her daughter, it's one hundred percent pure. She *wants* you to be in Skye's life."

"Okay, maybe you believe that, but she didn't even tell me

Skye might be mine. You had to be the one to figure it out. That's just—"

"Jacob," Brian said, cutting him off. "Sienna was here to offer you full custody of your daughter."

"What?" Jacob stood, suddenly no longer able to sit at the table. He paced the length of the kitchen. "You can't really be telling me that she was going to give up her daughter."

Brian stayed seated as he watched Jacob move back and forth in the dining room. "She's not well, Jacob. She wants what's best for Skye."

Jacob didn't know how to process that information. He already knew he needed his daughter more than air. But he couldn't imagine Sienna just signing away her rights to her child. That was truly insane. He paused and eyed Brian. And even as the words killed him, he forced out. "What about you? Is there a reason you're not what's best for her? Can't you take care of Skye while Sienna is getting treatment?"

"Are you saying you don't want full custody?" Brian asked, his eyes narrowed.

"No, that isn't what I'm saying at all. I want my daughter here with me always. I just want to understand the rationale and Sienna's mindset that would make her take such a drastic step."

"You want the cards on the table?" Brian asked.

"Yes," Jacob said. "All of them."

"Fine." Brian stood and started pacing just as Jacob had a few moments before. "Here's the truth. Sienna and I aren't a couple, and we never really were. We were sharing a house because of Skye, the little girl I *thought* was my daughter. I've been trying my damnedest to get Sienna help, but despite my best efforts, she seems to keep slipping. She knows it, too, so earlier this month, she went and got papers drafted that give you full custody." Brian pulled a folded contract out of his jacket pocket. "She had the papers drawn up in front of her therapist, who testified that she was of sound mind. All you have to do is sign, and you'll get full custody. The only thing she asks is that after she's well again, she'd like to be a part of Skye's life."

Jacob's hand shook as he took the papers from Brian and scanned them. The language was fairly standard. They were notarized and there was a letter attached from her therapist indicating that at the time that the papers were produced, Sienna wanted Jacob to have full custody. Jacob couldn't sign fast enough.

But as he pulled out his pen, he once again caught the pain in Brian's face and he set it back down. "Listen, man. I know how hard this must be for you."

"It's fine," Brian said, though his expression betrayed him.

"No, it isn't, brother."

"*Brother,*" Brian repeated, almost to himself. Then he raised his gaze and met Jacob's. "Brother's forever, man."

Jacob got up and indicated for Brian to follow him. They made their way into Skye's bedroom where she lay sleeping peacefully in the crib.

Brian stood there watching her for a moment. Then he leaned down, kissed her on the head, and whispered, "I love you, baby girl. Be good for your dad. You're lucky to have him."

"She's lucky she had you, Brian," Jacob said. When his friend turned to look at him, he added, "Thank you for watching over her and Sienna. I can't imagine where they'd be if you hadn't been there."

Brian shuffled his feet uncomfortably and then shrugged. "You'd have done the same for me."

Jacob pulled his friend into a hug and felt all of his resentment melt away. Whatever had happened in the past, it didn't matter now. Even though he hadn't seen it, his friend had never left him in spirit, and Jacob wouldn't ever leave him again.

When they broke the embrace, Jacob said, "I'm going to sign those papers today."

"I figured you would. Will you stay here?"

"Yes." Jacob glanced at his daughter. "It's a good place to grow up."

Brian nodded. "I know you always loved this place. Does the pretty brunette in the other room have anything to do with that decision?"

"Yes… and no," Jacob said with a smile. Just this morning he'd thought he had to leave her and the town he'd grown to love. But now… he was on the verge of getting everything he ever wanted. "Listen, Brian, how do you feel about being Skye's godfather?"

Brian, who'd been watching Skye sleep, jerked his head in Jacob's direction. "Are you serious?"

"It's obvious you love her. I can't imagine what that must've been like to believe she was yours and then find out she wasn't."

"I think I always kinda knew but didn't want to believe it." Brian brushed her curls out of her face. "But then when I knew… I couldn't do that to you or her."

Jacob smiled. "So, how about it?"

"I wouldn't have it any other way."

CHAPTER 26

Yvette sat with Skye across from her in one of the client rooms at Faith's soft opening for A Touch of Magic Day Spa. It was summer in Keating Hollow and the little girl had been in Jacob's life for a little over six months now. That entire time, she'd been nothing but a happy bundle of joy. Even now as they played, she was waving a stuffed turtle in the air and making giggling noises as if Yvette was the most entertaining person in the world.

"There you are," Jacob said from the doorway. "I was wondering what happened to my two best girls."

"Your only girls, I hope," Yvette said, smiling up at him.

"Well, there's the pair of you and Ms. Betty."

"Of course. You can't forget Ms. Betty. Is she still downstairs trying to get Hunter to give her a pelvic message?"

Jacob shuddered. "Last I heard, yes. But better him than me. At least she hasn't felt him up yet."

"*Yet* being the operative word," Yvette said.

Jacob got down on the floor and pulled Skye into his lap. The baby let out a loud cry of excitement. She turned in her father's arms to wrap her little hands around his neck and plant a watery kiss on his mouth.

Yvette's heart melted just like it did a million times a day when she saw them together. Jacob was the best dad, and the love between them was undeniable.

"I can't believe you three left me down there," Brian said as he strode into the room. "But I have to admit, hiding out while Ms. Betty is on a rampage is genius." About a month after Jacob had taken custody of Skye, Brian had rented a place and moved to Keating Hollow. He now spent at least half his time at Jacob's house and the two were as close as ever. Sienna was still working on herself, but she had been up to visit for two long weekends, and she and Jacob were making it work.

Skye heard Brian's voice and squirmed, trying to reach for him. He bent down and pulled her out of Jacob's arms. "I think my date is ready to make the rounds." He glanced down at her. "What do you say, Miss Skye? Ready to go make all the women fawn all over you?"

"Do not try to use my daughter to pick up women again," Jacob scolded, though the laugh lines around his eyes gave him away.

"I don't use her for anything. Is it my fault the ladies in the town find us irresistible?" He winked and strolled out of the room with Skye on his hip, the two of them making googly eyes at each other.

"He's a complete goner," Yvette said and grinned at Jacob. "Just like you. She has both of you wrapped around her little finger."

He snorted. "And what about you?" He glanced at the impressive pile of toys scattered around them. "I know at least a half-dozen of these are brand new. What do you do? Stock up on stuffed animals just to keep her entertained?"

"Yes, as a matter of fact I do," she said with a laugh. "Skye is a sucker for stuffed animals."

"And I'm a sucker for you." Jacob stood and held out his hand, and when she grabbed it, he helped her to her feet. "I wanted to ask you something."

"Okay, shoot. Is it something about the store?" Not long after Skye arrived, Jacob had stepped away from the bookstore, preferring to instead focus on being a stay-at-home dad. He was still a partner, and he and Yvette had regular meetings about what their plans were. But the day to day was all on her, which suited her just fine.

"Nope. Not the store." He lifted his hand and brushed a piece of hair behind her ear. "I was thinking that I'd really like to have you in my bed every night and every morning."

She laughed. "So, seventy-five percent of the time isn't good enough for you?"

He shook his head. "No, love. And Skye feels the same way."

Yvette narrowed her eyes at him. "Come on. She's one. Besides, I doubt she cares one bit if I'm in your bed."

"She cares if you're not there in the morning. You should've heard her screaming this morning." He shook his head as if he was still trying to clear the noise. "Full-on temper tantrum because her Vette wasn't there to feed her bananas."

"Did *you* feed her bananas?" Yvette asked.

"No." He slipped his arms around her waist and pulled her in close. "We ran out."

"Then there you go. She loves bananas best, and it's probably better if you just make sure you keep a good stock."

He rolled his eyes. "You sure know how to ruin a man's game."

"Game?" she laughed. "The only game you have these days, *Dad*, is the one where you toss dirty diapers into the correct receptacle."

Jacob threw his head back and laughed. "You know, I'd get upset about that, but it's true."

She shrugged one shoulder. "It's okay. I still think you're hot."

His eyes smoldered as he gazed down at her. "You do huh?"

Yvette nodded. "Definitely."

He tightened his grip on her waist and asked, "Would you say I'm hot enough to marry?"

She stiffened slightly at his words then blinked. "What did you just say?"

His lips curved up into a nervous smile as he pulled away from her and bent down on one knee.

Yvette sucked in a sharp breath. "This isn't what I think it is, is it? You're not really—"

Jacob pulled out a blue velvet box and opened it, revealing a very large, very shiny, solitaire diamond ring.

"Oh, my goddess," Yvette breathed with her heart racing a million miles an hour. She pressed her right hand to her chest while he took the left and slid the ring onto her ring finger. "You really are doing this."

"I am," he said softly, staring up at her with hope and possibility shining in his gorgeous eyes. "Yvette Townsend, will you marry me?"

Her throat ached, and her eyes burned, but for once she didn't try to hold back the tears. She stared at the ring then at Jacob. When her gaze landed on his, she saw the one and only man who made her heart and soul soar.

"Um, Yvette? An answer would be good here," he said, tightening his grip on her fingers.

She laughed through her tears and said, "Yes, Jacob Burton. I will so marry you. Anywhere, anytime. All I need is you and Skye."

He stood, still holding on to her hands and said, "Don't

think you're getting out of the big wedding. We're going to have the party to end all parties."

She groaned. "Seriously?"

Jacob shrugged. "That's debatable. Just as long as our friends and family are there."

This time she chuckled. "That would include the entire town."

"Exactly." He cupped both of her cheeks with both hands and stared into her eyes. "I love you, Yvette."

"I know," she said, smiling at him as her insides turned to complete mush. What had she ever done to deserve this man? She didn't know, but now that she had him, she was never letting him go. "I love you, too."

"Thank the gods," he said almost to himself. Then he wrapped her in his arms. "Remember what I said about Skye wanting you in my bed every night and morning?"

She nodded. "Yeah."

"I also have it on good authority that she'd like a little brother or sister. What do you think?"

Butterflies fluttered in Yvette's stomach as she gazed up at him and said, "I think we should start working on that tonight. What do you say?"

"I think that can be arranged," he said as if he hadn't just been looking at her like a wolf ready to eat his prey. "But first, we have to deliver some news." He walked over to the door and opened it. "After you, my love."

Yvette glanced down at the gorgeous ring sparkling on her finger and grinned. Her first try at marriage had ended spectacularly bad, but this time? This time she knew it was forever. She could feel it right down to her toes. She'd met her match in Jacob Burton, and he'd met his in her. She slipped her hand into his and said, "Ms. Betty's going to be really upset."

He nodded solemnly. "You know, you're probably right. Should I take my ring back and ask her instead?"

"Nah, you don't want to marry her. She's not nearly as talented as I am in the bedroom."

Both of Jacob's eyebrows shot up. "And you'd know this how?"

Yvette gave him an innocent smile. "I read her autobiography."

"She wrote an autobiography?" he asked. "You're joking, right?"

"Nope, not joking. And she's dedicated it to you. I left it on your night stand for some bedtime reading. She says there'll be a quiz later," Yvette added as she tugged him down the stairs to where their friends and family were celebrating Faith's spa opening.

"Now I know you're full of crap," he said with a laugh.

"Am I?" Yvette waved at the woman in question who was already making a beeline for them and tried not to laugh. "I guess there's only one way to find out."

"Why did I move to Keating Hollow?" he muttered under his breath.

"That's an easy one," she said as she gazed up at him. "It's because this place is magical."

His gaze locked with hers, and Yvette felt like they were the only two people in the room. Finally, Jacob said, "You're right. It *is* magical, and so are you. Now kiss me before Ms. Betty gets here."

"I thought you'd never ask."

DEANNA'S BOOK LIST

Pyper Rayne Novels:

Spirits, Stilettos, and a Silver Bustier
Spirits, Rock Stars, and a Midnight Chocolate Bar
Spirits, Beignets, and a Bayou Biker Gang
Spirits, Diamonds, and a Drive-thru Daiquiri Stand

Jade Calhoun Novels:

Haunted on Bourbon Street
Witches of Bourbon Street
Demons of Bourbon Street
Angels of Bourbon Street
Shadows of Bourbon Street
Incubus of Bourbon Street
Bewitched on Bourbon Street
Hexed on Bourbon Street

Witches of Keating Hollow:

Soul of the Witch
Heart of the Witch

Spirit of the Witch
Dreams of the Witch

Last Witch Standing:

Soulless at Sunset
Bloodlust By Midnight
Bitten At Daybreak

Witch Island Brides:

The Vampire's Last Dance
The Wolf's New Year Bride
The Warlock's Enchanted Kiss

Crescent City Fae Novels:

Influential Magic
Irresistible Magic
Intoxicating Magic

Destiny Novels:

Defining Destiny
Accepting Fate

ABOUT THE AUTHOR

New York Times and USA Today bestselling author, Deanna Chase, is a native Californian, transplanted to the slower paced lifestyle of southeastern Louisiana. When she isn't writing, she is often goofing off with her husband in New Orleans or playing with her two shih tzu dogs. For more information and updates on newest releases visit her website at deannachase.com.

Made in the USA
Columbia, SC
25 October 2018